SUTTON SOMEDAY

CAROLINE HOPKINS

UNTITLED

For additional information about this book and other Stratton Luce Media books, please email contact@strattonlucemedia.com

First Edition

ISBN 978-1-961878-05-1

UNTITLED

ONE

I had a test in physics on April 25th. I could clearly remember this, because I was awake late on the 24th, shuffling notecards into stacks, trying to stuff my brain with facts.

At 10:34 pm, I threw my physics notes to the side and walked into the kitchen to find a snack. My parents were out at a late dinner with my dad's co-workers, and I'd only had a piece of leftover pizza for dinner.

The house phone rang. That was weird, because the only person who'd call the house phone was my grandmother, who lived in Florida and was asleep by eight every night like clockwork.

Funny the small details you remember.

I stopped in front of the cordless phone. I never

answered the phone, but what if it was my grandmother? The line from the late night commercial, *help, I've fallen and I can't get up,* ran through my head.

I reached for the phone, holding it up to my ear. On the other end, I heard a click at the same time. My parents must have just gotten home, because I heard my mom's voice, slightly tipsy. "Hello?"

"Elaine Greer? This is Dartmouth Hitchcock Hospital."

I turned the corner. My mom was frozen in place, the phone in her hand, pressed against her face as though getting it physically closer was the older way to comprehend what was going on. "What?"

"Your daughter is in the hospital," the voice on the other end repeated. I didn't know why I hadn't put down the phone yet, just that it felt important to keep holding it.

"Sutton?" My mom's voice was too loud.

I couldn't blame her for the assumption. Bristol couldn't be in the hospital. The universe didn't work that way. My sister was the charmed one, who was never in trouble or unlucky.

"No, ma'am. Bristol. Bristol Greer."

My mom dropped the phone onto the kitchen floor. It bounced once and then lay still. My dad whipped around and sprinted to my mom, wrapping an arm to keep her up. "Elaine. Elaine. It's okay," he chanted, holding her.

I stood, rooted to the ground, still holding the other house phone to my ear. "Hello? Hello? Ma'am?" the voice called on the other end.

My dad walked my mom to a kitchen chair, reaching down and grabbing the phone. "What's going on?" he barked. He was a lawyer by training, and he knew how to call bullshit when I saw it. He would get to the bottom of this and make the world right again.

"Your daughter Bristol is at the hospital. She's in critical condition."

I pulled the phone away from my ear and slammed it back into its holder. It was impossible. It couldn't be.

I sprinted back to my room, like if I just went back to where I had been, the last few minutes hadn't happened. This had to be a dream. This couldn't be real.

A few minutes later, my mom arrived at my door, pushing it open without knocking. "Sutton." Her voice was clear, as though nothing had happened. "Your sister has had an accident. Your father and I are leaving for New Hampshire. Now."

Out the window, I saw my parents speed out the driveway on the five hour drive to Bristol's school. Two weeks later, I found a speeding ticket on the counter for going ninety-five on the highway near Boston.

They were gone for the next two days. My mom texted every few hours to make sure I was eating, but I knew that all her energy was caught up in Bristol. I was the daughter who was fine. I didn't need the extra help.

I didn't tell anyone that my parents were gone. It still didn't seem real. Bristol was happy and going to class and enjoying the first bit of spring in New Hampshire, and my parents were just visiting. It didn't make sense to me any other way.

At the end of the third day since the call, the car crept back into the driveway. I dropped my calculator on top of my math textbook and ran downstairs.

I waited for Bristol to come bounding through the door, to wrap me in a hug. But that didn't happen.

My parents opened the back door of the car, revealing a skinny, pale girl. She was wrapped in a Dartmouth sweatshirt three sizes too large and sweats. Her hair was stringy and loose, and she leaned on a crutch.

That couldn't be my sister. They must have picked up the wrong girl.

But as soon as I thought it, I saw her eyes flick up for a second, and I knew it was Bristol. But Bristol as I'd never seen her before.

"Sutton," my mom breathed as she walked closer, and I heard her silent entreaty. Stand aside, and let Bristol pass.

"We'll let you sleep downstairs for now, okay? So you don't have to navigate the stairs on your crutches." My dad's voice was low and quiet, aimed at Bristol.

They moved Bristol into the guest room on the first floor, and then came back to the kitchen. My mom had deep circles around her eyes, and my dad looked exhausted.

"What happened?" I asked, my voice quiet, as my dad rested his head against the fridge.

My dad looked over at me then turned away, his forehead leaving a mark on the stainless steel fridge. "Bristol," my mom started, then paused, staring down at the counters. "She tore her ACL."

I knew that. During lacrosse practice two weeks ago, Bristol had pivoted too fast and torn her ACL. In a single minute, she'd gone from being the team's top recruit to benched, potentially for the rest of college. I'd heard her coach on the phone with the doctor, figuring out how long it would take before she could play again.

But I knew Bristol. We all knew Bristol. She'd beat the doctors' estimates and be back in half the time they projected. By next season, she'd be back to being a phenomenon. That's who she was.

"She had a doctor give her pain medication for her ACL." My mom swallowed. "But she must have been in a lot of pain, because she took too much. Her roommate came home and called 911."

"She took too many pain meds?" That was impossible. Bristol wouldn't even take Tylenol when she had cramps during high school. She thought the pain made her stronger. I'd tried to raid her gym bag many times with no success.

My mom nodded. My dad turned towards me, clearing his throat. "We brought her home because Dartmouth isn't set up to have students on crutches. She'll recover better at home. And that way, her surgery will be here with a doctor we know."

I nodded. A car drove by on the street outside, its headlights momentarily lighting up my mom's face, where she stared into the space beyond me. Looking for her real daughter, maybe.

After that night, my house slipped further and further into silence. I doubled down, focused on my school work, and turned in my best semester of grades yet. I played soccer as though it would bring back the real Bristol.

Part of me hoped that if I turned in a winning soccer season, maybe it would somehow get back to Bristol, and she'd remember all of her lacrosse days and snap out of her slump. But our high school lost in the semifinals to our rival, and there was no trophy for me to bring home.

And Bristol stayed in her room. The neighbors asked about her. My mom smiled and told them how hard it was for competitive Bristol to be side-lined with an injury, but she'd be back at Dart-mouth in the fall. No one asked any more questions, because they all thought they all knew Bristol.

Like at one time, I thought I'd known my sister, too.

"HEY, babe, can you pass me my sunglasses?" Dylan asked, not looking up from his suitcase.

Summer vacation had just started, and I was helping my boyfriend of three months pack his things up for lacrosse camp. I reached over and passed him a pair of mirrored sunglasses, which were identical to the other pair of mirrored sunglasses hanging around his neck.

"Thanks, babe," he said, reaching for the t-shirts on his dresser, his back towards me.

I perched myself on the edge of his desk, still covered in old assignments from the end of the year. "So," I said, clearing my throat and feeling my heart start to stutter. "I'm going to miss you this summer."

"Why? I'm just going to lacrosse camp," Dylan replied, glancing up.

Because you're my boyfriend and you're going to be gone for two months, I wanted to say, but thought better of it. Dylan had his priorities straight. That was one of the things I liked about him. He liked me, but he knew that this was just another high school relationship.

I knew the statistics. High school relationships didn't make it through college. Even Bristol had broken up with her high school boyfriend. If she couldn't do it, I definitely couldn't.

"I'll be back at the end of the summer," Dylan replied. He pulled out a book from his suitcase, holding it up and examining it. "My mom stuck an SAT book in here. Seriously?"

"My mom left one on my dresser. I think she's trying to tell me something." The words slipped out before I could stop them, just keeping the conversation going.

It wasn't true. The one thing I was good at was

taking standardized tests. I found them strangely soothing. On multiple choice tests, there was always a right answer, and you just had to pick one. It wasn't like an essay or a paper, where I could spend hours making it perfect. No, it was A, B, or C.

But I'd tried to explain this to Dylan before, and he'd only stared at me with a blank look. "Sutton, that's weird.". I hadn't mentioned when I'd gotten my PSAT scores back and they'd come in higher than I expected – a whole twenty points higher than Bristol.

I still kept a copy of them in my room, buried under an old textbook so no one else would know. It had been unsettling to unwrap them and realize I'd beaten Bristol, like I was upsetting one of the essential laws of the universe.

"My priority is lacrosse. Obviously." Dylan finally stood up from his packing and looked at me. "I need to have a great season this year for recruiting when I get to college."

I nodded. That was one of the things that I liked about Dylan. He wasn't always exciting, but he was predictable. He had priorities.

"Speaking of," he said, zipping up his suitcase, "how's Bristol? Is she doing better after her surgery?"

"Yeah, she is," I said, catching myself looking down towards the floor. "She's recovering."

"That's good," Dylan said, unzipping his bag

slightly and putting in another pair of socks. "She'll feel better when she's back out and playing again. I know I would."

"Sutton?" Dylan's mom yelled as she walked up the stairs towards his room. "Dylan, I brought you some clean shirts."

"Thanks, Mom." Dylan grabbed the pile of clothes and dropped it on top of his dresser.

"I should probably head out." I meant it as a challenge. He was leaving for weeks. He should want to see me for longer.

Dylan turned and gave me a hug, kissing me on the forehead. "Bye, Sutton. See you in a couple months."

"Bye, Dylan." I glanced back at him as I headed down the stairs back out to my car. Through the front windows, I could see Dylan with his family, all of them gathered around his suitcase.

I started the drive back home and felt the urge, all of a sudden, to scream. Things with Dylan had seemed off lately, but not in any way I could put my finger on.

He'd asked me out for the first time right before spring break. I'd immediately gone home, hoping that Bristol would be home so I could ask for her thoughts. I'd waited on the front porch until her car pulled in, rocking on the porch swing.

"So," Bristol said as we walked into the house together. She dropped her bags and swung herself onto the counter, reaching over to the fridge and grabbing one of the flavored water my mom bought at Costco in pallets. "What's the hot gossip?"

"Am I really that transparent?" I asked.

"Yup," Bristol said, swinging herself down from the counter and grabbing another water, tossing one to me. Blackberry. It wasn't my favorite flavor, but Bristol loved it, and I'd never bothered telling my mom. "Spill."

"Dylan Walters asked me out." I bit my lip, then focused really intently on unscrewing the cap on my water.

"Dylan." Bristol narrowed her eyes. "Oh yeah, he's on the lacrosse team. Got it. He seems nice enough."

"Really? You're okay with him?" If Bristol liked him, I knew I was making the right choice.

"Are you asking for my approval? Seriously, Sutts?" Bristol grinned, taking a swig of her seltzer. "I mean, nothing could be worse than you crushing on Samuel Lawson. What a tool."

The year before I liked a guy who was on the student council with Bristol. He'd asked me out, then came over to watch a movie with me. We'd sloppily made out on the couch in the basement until Bristol came home. He'd jumped up and started to try to chat her up.

"I mean, he liked you, not me." Like most guys. She was a girl who any romantic comedy director would cast as the girl next door.

"And he was a jerk, so obviously neither one of us was going to waste our time with him." Bristol shook her head. "Sutton, the right guy is out there for you. I mean, maybe not in high school, but he's out there. If Dylan turns out to be the right guy, great. If not, I'll kick his ass."

And that had been all of the blessing that I'd needed to start dating Dylan. I never got butterflies in my stomach thinking about him, but I'd never really believed in those. Maybe in the movies. Maybe when I was in my twenties and living some impossibly glamorous life in New York. But not in high school. I didn't need that, anyway.

So I wasn't sure why I wanted to scream all of a sudden. "It's summer!" the DJ on the radio shouted. I reached down and flipped it off.

I spotted a pair of crutches lying next to the door as I walked in, the only sign that Bristol was home. She'd been home for six weeks, and I had still barely seen her.

"This is hard for your sister," was my mom's tight lipped response any time I said anything. "She can barely walk, so don't put more pressure on her. Please, Sutton."

So I hadn't. I hadn't commented when Bristol had refused to come out of her room for three weeks or when she didn't come to the soccer finals. I learned to accept things. Because that was all I could do.

TWO

By the fourth day of summer vacation, I had run out of things to look at on my phone. Dylan had sent me a grand total of three texts, and Bristol still hadn't come out of her room. Even Netflix had run dry.

I knew that I should be doing something productive, but I couldn't bring myself to. I'd read a page of my SAT book before I'd stuck it back in the shelf.

When we were kids, Bristol and I started summer break by watching old Disney movies. We'd pop popcorn in the microwave, more than once setting off the fire alarm and giving my mom a heart attack. We'd rewatch movies we'd seen a hundred times, throwing popcorn at the screen whenever a bad guy appeared.

That tradition had stopped when Bristol hit high

school. She was too busy with the things that mattered for college to watch kids' movies.

I spotted a stray bag of popcorn in the back of the kitchen cupboard. I could walk upstairs and knock on her door. But I couldn't imagine Bristol coming out of her room, let alone coming downstairs for a movie.

There was a letter on the kitchen counter from the town tennis courts, and I turned it over. It seemed sacrilegious to even think about going to the courts now – a ritual my sister and I shared that I wasn't inviting her in on, like watching a Disney movie alone. But it seemed even more like I'd ruin the memory of it if I asked her and she said no. I went to the front closet, dug out my old tennis racket, and threw it in the back of my car.

I drove to the town courts, which looked more run down than I remembered. I flashed my town park pass to the employee in the front, who barely looked up as I passed. It was good that they hadn't asked me what I was doing, because I still wasn't sure myself. I was just bored enough that anything was worth a try. At least it wasn't trying to study for the SATs.

I grabbed a ball from the ball basket and bounced it up and down on the court. I tossed the ball up and slammed it across the court, feeling my arm muscles come back. I played soccer for school normally, so anything with arms was beyond me

The ball slammed into the back wall rather than neatly landing in the middle of court. Disappointing. I grabbed another one and tried again. That one veered to the right and crashed into a pole.

Clearly I'd been misremembering how good I was at tennis. Maybe it was one of those memories that had become rosy with age, where now I remembered myself as a tennis champion rather than the solidly mediocre player I'd been. Or, I reminded myself, maybe I was just out of practice. I grabbed another ball, tossing it up and getting ready to hit it across the court.

Then I heard the shout from across the court.

"Heads up! Heads up! Oh my god, Alex, slow down!"

A tennis ball shot across the court, immediately followed by a blue blur.

I turned, trying to see what was going on. A person slammed into me. Not gently, but a full body slam. I staggered backwards, falling straight onto my butt.

"Oh god, I am so sorry."

My brain still hadn't processed everything that had happened. I was lying on the court, and my butt hurt. I looked up to see a guy my age leaning down towards me. His face was screwed up in concern, his eyebrows drawing together. "I mean it. I'm so sorry. That shouldn't have happened." His eyes lingered on mine for a second, then he turned his head. "Alex!"

The blue blur that had crashed into me turned out to be a small blond kid. The guy reached out and placed a hand on his shoulder. "What did I tell you about using other people's courts?"

"It's not my fault. Liam hit a ball over here and I had to come chase it!" The kid shook his head, crossing his arms and literally stamping his foot. He was a stereotype of an angry child right now. "I wasn't the one who hit it this time!"

The older guy rolled his eyes over the kid's head, then leaned down. "Alex. You were egging Liam on. Both of you showed bad judgment. Go find Natalie. I have to help the person you could have hurt."

Alex started walking away, stomping his foot with each step and dragging his racket on the court. "Don't do that!" the guy next to me yelled. "You're going to ruin it!"

Alex lifted the racket a fraction of an inch above the ground. The guy standing next to me ran his hand through his hair, his shirt riding up. He reached out his hand down towards me. "But seriously, I'm sorry."

I still couldn't figure out anything to say, other

than *it was the kid's fault, not yours.* He wrapped his fingers around mine and pulled me up. It was a weird sensation, sending what could have been butterflies down through my stomach. I dropped my hand away as soon as I was fully standing.

For the first time, I looked closely at him. He looked vaguely familiar, but I couldn't place him – he could have easily been one of the guys in my English class, or freshman year social studies, or any other class that I'd mostly forgotten.

"Do I know you?" he asked, his gaze not leaving my face. "I'm pretty sure we've met."

I was used to this. "Sutton Greer," I said, sticking out my hand to shake and then thinking better of it. We weren't congratulating each other on sportsmanship.

"Oh, hey." His eyes widened, and I braced myself for the inevitable questions. *Oh, I heard about your sister, how's she doing?* But they didn't come. "You play soccer, right?"

"Yeah, I do," I replied.

"I thought I recognized you. I'm Michael Shipman." He stuck his hands into his pockets, his eyes still on my face.

Michael Shipman. Of course. Everyone in the neighborhood knew his story. Michael's dad had been the phenomenally popular head of the youth lacrosse program. Four years ago, he'd died in an accident. He'd been driving home from work on the interstate, and a tired truck driver hadn't seen him changing lanes. He was killed instantly.

According to the gossip, the Shipman family had fallen apart after that. Michael had refused to return to regular school, cutting every class. He'd been sent to boarding school after cutting class. He'd come back to my school last year and refused to even talk to the lacrosse coach. Everyone was expecting him to pick up the family sport and give us all an inspirational comeback story. But he hadn't.

"I haven't seen you here before," he said, reaching down towards the ball bucket. He grabbed a ball, tossing it up into the air and catching it without looking.

"I thought I'd come out for the day." My face started to flush. I'd planned to come out and play with the retirees, not people my age. "I mean, I didn't have much else to do. My sister and I used to play during the summer, until she got busy with high school stuff." I could feel myself starting to ramble as I said it. I wasn't even sure why I'd decided to pick today to hit tennis balls, and now I had to explain it to someone else. Someone attractive, not that I noticed that much.

"You're pretty good for someone who claims that

you just play once in a while," Michael replied, continuing to toss and catch the ball without looking.

I blushed before I could stop myself. "Do you play? Normally, I mean, not just now.," I asked.

"Not for school or anything." Michael kept tossing the tennis ball, one side of his mouth twisting up into a smile again. His eyes met mine and I blushed again. I figured that it had to be the heat. "I'd play if you wanted to, but normally I teach at the camp here."

"There's a tennis camp here?" Of course there was. That would be why there were so many kids running around. Something about Michael's presence was making me say stupid things.

He raised his eyebrows at me. "You're telling me that you never went to camp here? You're too good to have skipped the Twelve to Love program."

I should have known that our town had a cutesy name for the tennis program. This was the town that named its park the Greenville Greenway. "Hit that well? I just spent the last five hits slamming the ball into the back wall."

"You have plenty of power," he said, glancing at where the tennis balls were lying on the ground. "But you can actually control the ball, too. Most people hit the ball somewhere random. You know how to keep things under control."

"You clearly are seeing some other girl's tennis skills." I looked over at where I'd hit my first few shots. They'd been in bounds, but only technically.

I'd never been good at tennis to start with. Bristol and I played together because it had been fun. We hadn't ever practiced enough to be good. I knew as well as anyone that you couldn't be good at something without pain and suffering.

"I'm serious! We should play sometime." He smiled and then glanced away over my head, the hint of a dimple starting to show on his right cheek. "Do you want to come say hi?"

Another stray ball landed on my court. I wasn't going to play with all this commotion anyway, so I might as well. "Alex!" Michael shouted. "Stop that!"

"I'll come," I said, surprising myself. Tennis was something I'd tucked away with all my memories of Bristol. It seemed wrong that I was here without her. But if she wasn't going to come with me, I might as well go myself.

"Well, come on," he said, starting to reach his hand towards me and then pulling it back, pointing towards the court ahead of us. "That way, I can make Alex properly apologize for attempting to push you over earlier."

"Heads up!" Michael shouted as we walked into

the next court. A dozen eight year olds whipped around to look at Michael. "Rackets down!"

All dozen kids dropped their rackets to their sides at once. They made a clanking noise as they all fell down to the ground, and the kids turned around to look at me. I blushed again.

"They're showing off for you," a girl said from beside me. She was my age, but wearing a bright blue t-shirt that read Greenville Tennis and eyeshadow that matched her shirt. "I've never seen them get this quiet before, even when I threatened them with a dinosaur attack."

"Sutton here," Michael said, pointing towards me, "has kindly agreed to show you guys how to hit a ball with some control. Alex, I highly recommend you pay attention."

"I'm doing what?" I asked, glancing at the girl beside me as though she had an explanation for what was happening. I was just coming to get an apology.

She rolled her shoulders. "They're getting out of control, and they seem to like you, so I guess Michael's just throwing spaghetti at the wall. Metaphorically speaking, of course."

"Throwing spaghetti?"

"Yeah. You know how if you throw spaghetti at the wall and it sticks, you know that you've cooked it all the way? You're the spaghetti," she said, now swinging her arms in giant circles.

"I've never heard of throwing spaghetti to see if it sticks." There was no way that my mom would have let anyone throw things at her kitchen walls. And I wasn't sure I liked being compared to pasta.

"It's a thing," she assured me. "Patented method."

"Sutton!" Michael called again. His eyes met mine for a second. "Take the far side of the court, and let's show these kids how it's done."

I looked at the girl next to me. She shrugged again, reaching for her water bottle and taking a drink. "I'm not qualified for this," I said.

"Michael gave you his vote of confidence, not me," she said. I couldn't tell if her tone was jealous or not, but I wondered for a second if I'd accidentally stumbled into something. I had never learned how to tell if someone liked someone else from a distance.

It was clear that no one was coming to bail me out, so I took my racket and jogged over to the other side of the court. Michael lobbed the first serve towards me. I hit it back and it landed straight in the middle of the court.

"I told you that you were good," he called back to me. I shrugged. Beginner's luck. He tossed another one, and it hit in exactly the same spot.

He was clearly making this easy for me. I'd never done this well with Bristol. Bristol and I had had a game, a redemption game that I was allowed to use when the dishes total got too high, where we'd pick a spot on the court and whoever could hit it the most times in a row got off dish duty for a week. Usually we'd leave her shoe in the middle of the court, and she'd always throw the game so that I could get out of dish duty.

"Okay," Michael said, pointing down towards the court. "Right here on the paint. How many times in a row can you get it there?"

That was too easy. Bristol and I hadn't done something as simple as a corner in years. I returned his first serve there, and then the next, then the next. It felt good to just hit the ball again, the thunk as my racket connected with it.

I stopped, feeling the muscles in my arms again. It felt good to do something different than my drills for soccer. I looked back over my shoulder. The girl with blue eyeshadow and the kids were all staring at me. I stared around, then dropped my racket to my side.

I wasn't good at tennis. I had no idea where that had come from.

Michael stared at me for a second, his eyes boring into mine. I swallowed. He dropped the last ball onto the ground. "And that is control." He dragged his eyes away from me over towards the kids. "That's it for today. Natalie and Nora will take you out to meet your parents."

The girl with the blue eyeshadow waved at the kids as though she was attempting to flag down a passing helicopter. The kids all started to walk towards her. Alex pushed some other kid, who pushed him back, and she had to separate them.

"Sutton. That was awesome." Michael jogged over to me, stopping directly in front of me and pushing his hair back from his forehead. He must have seen my look, because he shook his head. "No, seriously, Sutton. I'd like to play with you. You're way better than I am, and the kids love you. I've never seen them shut up for someone before."

"I don't know. I'm not really a tennis player," I said, reaching up and tightening my ponytail. I'd always lost playing against Bristol, so today must have just been a streak of really good beginner's luck.

"Whatever you say. The offer still stands." Michael shrugged, and his eyes traveled back to mine, lingering for a second too long. He cleared his throat, pushing his hair back again. "I have to clean up the balls, but I'll see you around."

He jogged off. I stared after him for a second, watching him gather up all the tennis balls we'd hit.

Then I picked up my racket and headed towards the club building. This felt like a good time to stop, like the universe had given me all the luck that I was going to get for today.

"Okay, Sutton Greer, explain what the hell you were doing out there," said a voice behind me. I whipped around to see the smiling face of Stacey Chapman.

Stacey was my best friend freshman year. We'd met during orientation, when we'd been separated into our homerooms for the first time. There had been an introductory speech about how wonderful high school could be if we didn't drink too much or do drugs or get pregnant and ruin our lives, followed by a snack break with only packets of carrots.

Stacey had been sitting at the desk next to me and turned to face me, holding up her package of baby carrots. "I'm all for being healthy and all, but remember when we got cupcakes on the first day of kindergarten?"

I blushed, which was my normal response to having anyone new talk to me. Fortunately, Stacey kept talking. "And high school is way more stressful than kindergarten, so if we deserve sugar at any point, it's definitely today," she continued, waving her tiny package of carrots around.

I cleared my throat and forced the words out.

"Are you sure Mrs. Morales didn't have cupcakes as one of those things we had to avoid in high school?"

"Probably!" Stacey grinned, then reached over and shook my hand, like it was a totally natural way to make friends now that we were in high school. "Cupcakes. Sounds fun. Must warn students against them. I'm Stacey, by the way."

"I'm Sutton," I said, feeling the intense relief that I hadn't been too weird yet.

"S squared! So what's your schedule?" Two minutes later, Stacey and I were making plans on where we'd meet to sit in the cafeteria.

She and I were inseparable freshman year. Then we drifted apart sophomore year. We had different classes that year, so it was only logical we had different study groups, and different sports on top of it. Junior year, I'd taken as many AP classes as I could, and the precious little bit of free time I had was eaten up by soccer.

It was one of those friendships where I couldn't pinpoint an end to it. There were some friends where I could do that – we'd hit fifth grade, or eighth grade, or high school, and the other girl had changed. They'd become the popular ones, while I'd stayed in the background. There were party invitations I'd turned down, inside jokes I didn't understand any more, and the friendship had broken.

Stacey and I were just drifting apart, slowly but irrevocably.

But now here she was, looking the same as ever. She was grinning, like it was freshman orientation again. "Stacey! It's been forever."

"Trust me, Sutton Greer." Stacey had always been a fan of using first and last names for emphasis. "It's been a year and a half. I have a great memory for that sort of thing." She wasn't kidding – she could name the outfit every person at our high school was wearing the day she'd first met them. Apparently I'd been wearing a yellow sundress with flowers on it. "What are you doing here, and where've you been hiding?"

I'd been hiding in my house, alongside Bristol, both refusing to come out of our rooms. But I wasn't sure that we were close enough for me to say that. I shrugged. "I came to hit around, and then I got dragged into helping Michael out with the kids."

"You were at tennis camp? No way!" Stacey's whole face lit up. "That's why I'm here. I run the program. I mean, Michael and Nora and Natalie actually teach the kids, but I'm the responsible one who calls the parents and handles the paperwork."

That didn't surprise me. Stacey had given up track to manage the girls' basketball team sophomore year, and she'd been amazing at it. "And what do you mean, you got dragged into helping?" Stacey placed a hand on her hip and gave me the look she'd always given me when I was holding back some choice piece of gossip.

"One of the kids ran onto my court, and Michael invited me to show them how I hit," I replied.

"Oh yeah, you and Bristol used to come here all the time! You were really good," she said. I waited for a comment about Bristol, but none came. "Honestly, I was surprised when you took up soccer instead of tennis."

Stacey's phone rang, and she glanced down, her nose wrinkling. "These parents are pushy. I should never have given out my number. Text me later, okay? I'd love to hit sometime. It's been too long."

I nodded, relieved that she was making the first move. I wouldn't have to figure out what was cool and what was too much to invite her to. I headed towards the exit when I heard another voice calling me. "Control girl!"

I turned around to see the girl with blue eyeshadow waving at me, using both her arms above her head. "Sutton! I totally know your name. I've totally seen you around school, but I just big time blanked. Too much time in the sun." She pointed to herself, then to the girl next to her. "Natalie, and Nora."

The girl sitting next to Natalie waved. She was wearing a t-shirt from last year's homecoming, her hair in a bun. She had one of those sunburns that looked like it was about to start peeling any minute, and I almost wanted to dig in my bag to find some aloe vera for her.

Natalie and Nora. Another couple of girls at school where I knew their names and a few things about their lives. I knew that Natalie threw up at a third grade birthday party, and that Nora had gotten kicked out of biology for refusing to dissect a frog, but that was it. Only the surface things about them.

"You've come just in time for the most important part of summer," Natalie said, clapping her hands together.

"Nat, you have got to take off that eyeshadow. Please, I'm begging you." Nora closed her eyes, tipping her head back towards the ceiling. "It's actually making my eyes hurt."

Natalie fist pumped. "I told you if you made more than three comments about my eyeshadow, you were buying my ice cream today, so pay up, loser." She turned towards me. "I'm trying to teach Nora to be a nicer person."

"I am a nice person. I'm just honest, and that is the worst possible color for your complexion," Nora said, reaching for her water bottle.

"Ignore Nora," Natalie declared, clapping her hands together again. "More importantly, Sutton, you are about to witness the most important part of any summer. The summer bucket list."

I tried to make my face seem excited. I had never been a fan of the idea of bucket lists. It sounded so limiting, and I wasn't even sure what I would put on what. Go to college, probably, but I was going to do that anyway.

Nora leaned forward, resting her forearms on the counter. "Every summer, Nat and I make a bucket list."

"And once something's on the bucket list, you have to follow through. It's a crime against our friendship to refuse to do something on the bucket list," Natalie finished. She caught sight of her reflection in the window across from us and shook her head. "Okay, Nora, you're right about the eyeshadow. I still won the ice cream though."

"Check out what we've got so far," Nora said, sliding a crumpled sheet of notebook paper across the counter towards me. I picked it up and read:

Try every ice cream flavor at Brittany's. Even the rainbow sherbet.

Go berry picking and make something edible after. In different handwriting: *Nora, that means not setting your kitchen on fire this year!*

Steal pants from Charles Huntington the Third. Ideally the red cords with light bulbs embroidered on them. Maybe to explain this one, there were doodles of pants all over the sides of the list.

Party at the Orchards

Go skinny dipping

Sneak out at midnight to meet a boy! Extra points if you have to go out a window.

"Isn't it a solid list?" Natalie asked, craning her neck towards me. "We could probably use a few more items, but it's the perfect mix of refined and ridiculous."

"You're stealing some guy's pants?" It felt like an oddly specific item to put on your bucket list, as well as a crime.

"Not just any guy." Nora closed her eyes, as though saying this was bringing back too many memories. "Charles Huntington. He was unfortunately my boyfriend earlier this year. And if you think Nat's eyeshadow is bad, you should see his pants."

"They hurt my eyes. I had to wear sunglasses around him," Natalie added.

"But seriously, the worst pants. He took every stereotype you could have of a kid with the third in his name and embraced it. He had one pair of khakis covered in giant pastel triangles."

"The pink paisley ones!" Natalie shook her head. "Those were extra awful."

"He wore them to dinner with my sister. She told me she cut her lip because she had to keep biting it not to laugh. We're doing this town a favor if we steal his pants," Nora finished.

"And then ritually burn them." Natalie crossed her arms and stared directly at me for emphasis.

"I was going to donate them to charity." Nora shrugged, reaching up and tucking a single stray piece of hair into her bun. "Earn him some better karma."

"I'm all for donating to charity, but those pants are so ugly that they'll make anyone who gets them sadder. We're burning them, at the beach, in honor of the time he ditched you because his parents told him he could get a drink with alcohol in it at the yacht club," Natalie replied.

"The guy was a real winner." Nora shook her head and walked over to a cooler on the ground nearby, grabbing three sports drinks and tossing one to each of us. "Are you dating anyone, Sutton?"

"Uh, yeah." I knew that people talked about their significant others all the time, but it never felt like I had anything interesting to say about Dylan. Everyone at school already knew him, and it wasn't like I knew some version of Dylan that no one else did. With Dylan, what you saw was what you got. "Dylan Walters."

"Oh. That's – that's nice." Nora nodded. "Good for you."

"Dylan Walters?" Natalie's eyebrows had shot up practically to her hairline. "He's such a prick. He takes himself way too seriously. How do you put up with that?"

"Nat!" Nora said, shooting her a glare that could have melted ice.

"Sorry, sorry," Natalie said, throwing out her hands to the side and then looking over at me. "I tend to blurt things out, and half the time they're not nice. I'm sure he's a wonderful guy when you get to know him." She glanced at Nora. "Better, Nora?"

"I'm not offended," I said quickly. I realized a second later that I should have jumped in with some anecdote about Dylan to prove my point – he could be sweet, and he cared about his future, and he was driven. But for some reason, I couldn't find the right words to say.

"Let's focus here, girls." Nora lifted the summer bucket list up again, pinching a corner of it between her pointer finger and thumb.

Natalie chugged her drink, then dropped the bottle on the ground. "Skinny dipping has to be on there, I don't care what you say. It is a seminal high school experience, and you live next to the beach."

"I told you, I'll do it. I don't mess around with the rules of the summer bucket list," Nora replied. "Even if I did originally propose a midnight swim in our bikinis."

"Not like there will be people around, so who cares?" Natalie turned towards me. "Sutton, you in?"

Everything on that list was the opposite of what I had planned my summer to be. I was going to work at the internship my parents had gotten for me, I'd practice soccer, I'd fix things with Bristol.

For a second, some part of my brain wanted to throw all that away and do it. But that wasn't me. Maybe in some other universe I'd be that girl, but I shook my head, distancing myself another inch from the counter where Natalie and Nora sat. "Sounds awesome, but I'm slammed with stuff this summer."

"Your loss," Natalie said, shrugging. I couldn't tell whether she was offended, and I fought the impulse to make some sort of self-deprecating comment so she knew I didn't mean it personally. That list just wasn't who I was.

"I should probably head out. My parents are probably wondering where I am," I said. That was a total lie – my parents knew that I was mature and adult, that I'd be home on time and honor all my promises. But I didn't know how to walk away without offending them any other way. "It was great to see you."

"Yeah, come back. I've never seen the kids shut up for so long." Natalie grinned and tightened her ponytail. "See you around, Sutton."

THREE

"Sutton?" My mom rounded the corner into the kitchen as I finished shoveling down a yogurt. It was my first day of my summer this-will-look-good-for-college internship, and I was desperately trying not to spill anything on my top. "Oh good, you're ready to go. I just wanted to wish you good luck."

"Okay," I managed, swallowing a mouthful of yogurt.

My mom's eyes crinkled in the corner for a second, and I swore I could see her relax for a nanosecond. "I know you're going to do so well at this." She reached over and gave me a completely unexpected hug.

I hugged her back, then headed out towards the car. I arrived at the offices of Bethany Carlson, Esquire, fifteen minutes later.

Bethany was one of my mom's friends. She was as always impeccably dressed. Even her office looked like something that you would see on Instagram, white walls, polished concrete floors, trendy wire chairs, and artistically arranged plants in the corner.

I walked in the door and waited for a second, looking around. My polyester blouse had already soaked through with the humid heat outside, and now it was clinging to my skin in the air conditioning.

"Sutton, welcome!" Bethany came out of the back room, her perfectly manicured hands wrapping around a steaming cup of coffee. Her hair had already been blown out this morning. "I'm so glad that you're here. We loved having your sister."

"Thanks. I'm excited to be here, too." Bristol had been Bethany's intern a few years ago. Bethany had even written a glowing letter to Dartmouth about Bristol's professionalism and work ethic. My mom was worried that my college application wouldn't stand out, so she'd called in a favor to make sure I got the same internship as Bristol did.

"I was hoping to give you more of an introduction, but I have a very busy day." Bethany looked around the room we were standing in, still holding her coffee in both hands. She stared at one of the plants for a second, her eyes narrowing, then back towards me. "My paralegal can show you how to file paperwork and answer phone calls when she needs to step away."

I nodded, my blouse clinging to my front more now. I wanted to reach around and unstick it from my skin, but I didn't know how to do that without looking completely out of place. Bethany didn't seem like the kind of woman who sweat.

"So your desk will be in the back office," Bethany said, starting to walk down a hallway out of the lobby. I followed her. There were modern art pieces on each wall, artistic swirls of color against the white walls.

She stopped at the end of the hallway. She pointed to a windowless room, a giant monitor sitting on top of a desk, facing the wall. I walked in, setting my bag down on the chair. She smiled at me, the smile not quite reaching her eyes. "For today, I'd like you to scan in the mail that we've received in the past year and add it to our shared drive. I'm sure you can figure out how the scanner works."

"I can do that." It was a scanner, after all. It wasn't that difficult. Part of me had been hoping that it would be something more interesting - research, maybe, or having to file interesting things. But scanning was good enough.

"The instructions for what you should do each day are in that binder on your desk, and Andrea will give you any special projects or answer any questions that you have." And with that, Bethany gave me one last cold smile, then turned on her heels and walked away.

I took a deep breath and sat down at the desk, turning on the computer in front of me. I looked at the neat stack of papers on either side of the desk, which looked like a stack of utility bills. I could faintly hear Bethany's voice on the phone, barely audible over the whooshing of the air conditioning. I stood up and started paging through the binder.

It took a solid three hours before I had already decided that this wasn't going to be a job I loved. All I had done was scan in several years of utility bills. Bethany didn't stop for lunch, so I sat down and unwrapped my granola bar at my desk, staring at my phone.

Despite the temperature outside, I was freezing cold in this office. I should have brought headphones, because the only noise in here was the hum of the air conditioning machine.

I didn't want this for the summer, said the tiny voice in the back of my head. But of course, this was what you did to prepare for college. "Sutton, this is a great opportunity," my mom had said at dinner the night I'd gotten the internship.

"I don't know." I didn't know the right words to explain what I was feeling, so I settled for vague phrases. "It just doesn't feel like me."

My parents' faces shifted into their We Are Being Reasonable With Our Teenager look. There had to be some parenting book somewhere with instructions on how to do it. "Sutton," my dad said, "Bristol did this internship, and it helped her get into college. You have to consider your future."

My mom followed up immediately. "I know it might be hard for you to imagine having a job instead of having a free summer, but it's part of growing up, Sutton. Think about college."

I didn't know how to object, so I had nodded and stuffed my mouth with more salad. This was going to be my summer, scanning documents in a quiet room. I didn't know what I had pictured for my summer, but it wasn't this.

I stuffed the rest of the granola bar into my mouth, listening to the silence for a second. Five hours of this to go. I tossed the wrapper into the trash can and picked up the next document to scan.

.   .   .

THREE DAYS LATER, I found myself unexpectedly aimless. Bethany was at a conference and closed the office for the day. It was probably a test of some sort, but I couldn't bring myself to promise to go in when she wasn't there.

Which meant that I had to find something to do. As soon as I had any amount of time to myself, I found myself sleeping or surfing the internet, trying to fill up the emptiness in the house.

I sat at the kitchen counter, stirring a bowl of yogurt. The house was completely silent, with only the drip of the coffeemaker and the occasional passing car to break it up. It took me a bit to realize what I was missing, the noise of the tennis courts.

I left a note on the counter to let my mom know where I was going, then headed out. My tennis racket was still in the backseat of my car from the week before, looking lonely in the back set.

I pulled up to the courts and saw a car with track and field bumper stickers next to an open spot. My heart skipped a couple beats. I parked before I could get any more nervous and possibly bump into the car. I'd failed my driving test the first time when I got nervous and hit the gas too hard, and I wasn't going to repeat that.

I walked towards the front desk, digging through

my bag for my membership card, when I heard the voice. "Sutton!" Michael was walking out towards me, wiping his face with a towel. "What's up?"

My heart stuttered. I had known that I might see him here, but it was different in person. "I was wondering," I cleared my throat, hoping I wasn't blushing, "if the offer to play still stood."

Michael grinned, the sort of grin that snuck from one corner of his mouth to the other. "It absolutely still stands. Even if you're fresh and rested and I just played."

"Oh, cool!" I was definitely blushing now. "I mean, I didn't know if you were being serious when you said that, so just in case."

"Of course I meant it. I want to play with you." He stuffed his sweat towel into his bag. "Let's go."

I followed him out to the courts, my heart hammering. It was nerve wracking to have to play a sport I didn't know if I was good at. I didn't like not being good at things, especially when there was an attractive person on the other side of the court.

Within five minutes of scrimmage, I could feel how out of shape I was. My arm ached as I reached around, trying to return Michael's perfectly on point serve. He might claim he wasn't good at this, but he was good at this.

"That was awesome. You're really good at this," Michael said right after he landed the winning shot. It had been just out of my reach, and I wasn't quite at the point where I'd throw myself on the ground to catch every single possible return. I'd done that with Bristol many times, and ended up going home covered in scrapes. After enough lectures from my mom about safety –"isn't tennis supposed to be a no contact sport" – I'd eventually stopped.

"You know I'm not paying you to give me false compliments, right?" I rubbed my arm, as though that was going to ward off the soreness tomorrow.

"You know that's not actually part of my job, right?" Michael asked, bouncing a ball up and down off the court. "I teach people how to play better. When I tell them that they're good at this, it's because they are."

"Why are you coaching?" The town wasn't known for paying well for summer jobs, and he was Michael Shipman. Any of the private lacrosse camps would have paid him triple this to just show up.

Michael flicked a piece of hair back away from his face. "It's an easy way to make some money. I get to work out while getting paid, and it's not like cross country has a camp I have to go to. And most of the people I coach are pretty cool."

"I haven't been going to soccer practice this summer," I said, the words spilling out. Technically they were optional practices, and the coach had told us that we didn't need to go if we trained on our own. My parents thought that I was there every day, but I'd skipped the first one and couldn't bring myself to go to the next one.

"That doesn't seem like you," Michael said, tossing a ball into the air and catching it without looking.

"What do you mean?"

"You're so serious all the time. At school you're always focused on your notes, or soccer, or whatever, and I don't think I've ever seen you laugh."

His eyes met mine, and my stomach did something that wasn't exactly butterflies. It was more of a half flip, a synchronized swimming routine.

Michael was good looking enough that I felt guilty for noticing. People wouldn't swoon and blush when he walked by the hallway, but I couldn't help but notice the bulge of his arm muscles as he hit the ball idly.

I shouldn't have been noticing anything about how Michael looked, though, since I was with Dylan. Dylan, who'd texted me once in the past three days. Dylan, who still didn't know about my sister.

"Michael, your ten o'clock is here!" someone called from across the court.

Whatever moment there was, if there was anything that even qualified as a moment between us, was gone. Michael tore his eyes away from mine, tossing the tennis ball up and down again. "So," he said, still not looking right at me but continuing to toss the tennis ball, "can we make tennis a regular thing?"

My heart skipped for a second and I swallowed before answering. It suddenly felt ten degrees warmer outside. "Sure. I mean, once my arms recover from today. That was the most tennis I've played in years."

For a second Michael turned more towards me, and we made brief eye contact. He smiled down towards me. "What's your number?" he asked, reaching for his phone.

Calm down, said the voice in the back of my head. *He just wants a tennis partner, and anyway, you have Dylan. Remember him?*

I reached for his phone and tapped it in, feeling the slickness of his phone case from his sweat. It felt too personal again, holding his phone, warm from his hands. "In there."

"I'll text you," he said, starting to jog backwards towards the other side of the court. "Now off to show another ten year old how to control a tennis ball."

I laughed again, the sound feeling weird. He waved, then turned and jogged off in the direction of his next lesson.

I walked back to the front of the clubhouse, already feeling the ache start in my arm. Michael was good, maybe even better than Bristol. I paused at the water fountain to take a drink. "I thought I saw Sutton out there earlier," a high female voice said, and I stopped. Someone was in the clubhouse, talking about me. It sounded like Natalie.

I paused with that guilty but curious feeling I always got when I overheard people gossiping. I wanted to know, but I felt like I should be honest and come out and tell them I was here. It wasn't fair to judge them on something that they might never say to my face. It was the sensation of being guilty by being in the wrong place at the wrong time, of over-hearing what other people shouldn't have said.

"She's good," replied a second, lower voice, which had to be Nora.

"I mean, why doesn't she play tennis instead of soccer? Or at least play lacrosse, you know?"

I knew what was coming here. Some variation on "her sister was so good at it, why doesn't Sutton try?". People saw Bristol and were convinced that as her sister, I must magically be good at lacrosse and school and popular. I felt guilty sometimes for squandering the imaginary genetic gift I'd been given.

"I mean, it has to be the same muscles," Natalie continued. "Waving around a six foot metal pole and a tennis racket can't be that different, can they?"

After years of hearing lacrosse described as an incredibly complex sport, with a rich history and sophisticated tactics, the realization that my sister was famous for waving around a giant metal stick made me burst out laughing.

"Hello?" Natalie rounded the corner to find me. I swallowed, trying to get the laughter to stop. It wasn't even that funny. It was just that lacrosse had always been such a mythical thing in my house, and it was like I'd finally burst that bubble. "Sutton, I thought I saw you!"

"Yeah, sorry, I just got a funny text." I swallowed again, finally getting the laughter to stop.

"Well, Nora and I are going to head out for ice cream at Brittany's if you want to come," Natalie said, tightening her ponytail.

"Thanks, but I have to get home," I replied automatically, the same words I'd used for every invitation since Bristol came home.

Natalie shrugged. "Guess I'll see you around then."

I walked out to my car and put the tennis bag in the back. It wasn't that I didn't want to be friends with Natalie and Nora so much as that I didn't know how to be. Friends had always been something that seemed to come automatically along with a sport. Bristol had lacrosse friends. I had soccer friends.

Those were the kinds of friends that took no effort to explain. They were my friends because we had something in common. But I'd never been able to talk to them about serious things. We talked about school and soccer and our exams, but I didn't know any of them better than I knew Natalie and Nora. I knew things about them, but I didn't know them.

I turned the car on, staring out the windshield. The thought of the house filled me with a strange loneliness, and I turned right instead of left, heading towards the beach and Brittany's.

The beach was already packed with families when I arrived. I circled the parking lot twice, finding the last spot that didn't require parallel parking. I got out and headed towards Brittany's, pushing my car keys into my pocket.

"Sutton! You came after all!" Natalie said, doing another of her air traffic controller waves.

"Yeah, I did," I said. I still wasn't quite sure what had compelled me to follow them. "Ice cream."

"Ugh, I think it's my day for mint chocolate chip.

I should get this over with," Nora said, staring at the flavor board.

"Over with?" I asked. Mint chip wasn't my favorite, but it was one of the more standard flavors here. Brittany's had been our reliable beachside ice cream shack for years, since my parents were kids. It had served chocolate, vanilla, and variations on those themes for years.

Then the owner had gone into semi-retirement. His daughter had left culinary school in New York to run the place, and she had brought with her new ice cream flavors.

Really strange ice cream flavors. I liked vanilla and chocolate chip cookie dough and rocky road. I didn't understand why people tried to put vegetables in ice cream. If you were eating ice cream, you were already admitting that you weren't trying to be healthy. Ice cream was another one of those things that was best left as it was.

"It's one of our summer bucket list items," Natalie explained, pointing towards the flavor board hanging over the ice cream counter. "We're trying all twenty-six flavors here."

"Which unfortunately includes mint chocolate chip," Nora finished, turning away from the flavor board to face me. "I would rather eat a worm than something mint flavored."

"But mint's so basic. It's basically vanilla," I said. And nothing with chocolate chips in it could ever be that bad.

"I hate all things mint," Nora crossed her arms over her chest. "A lot."

"Like, the first time she came for a sleepover at my house, forgot her toothpaste, and all I had was mint flavored one. She wouldn't brush her teeth." Natalie raised an eyebrow towards me.

"It's disgusting," Nora replied.

"She once gagged after kissing Tyler Matson – not because he's lame, but because he was chewing mint gum," Natalie whispered, loud enough for everyone to hear.

"Natalie, I thought we'd agreed not to talk about that." Nora's arms were even more tightly crossed now, her eyes starting to narrow.

"And candy canes? Don't even start." Natalie shook her head, her ponytail flying back and forth. Her ponytail had tiny pink tips, like she'd dyed her hair and never quite cut the ends off. "Seriously, she's like the Grinch. No Christmas spirit."

"I would have more Christmas spirit if people didn't try to ruin Christmas by making its symbol the grossest candy ever. Peppermint patties and candy canes. It's an onslaught for us mint hating people." Nora sighed and stared back at the board, then looked over at Natalie. "Did we really write every flavor? Not just the flavors we don't already know we hate?"

"That's cheating," Natalie said firmly, crossing her arms to match Natalie. They stared at each other for a few beats, then Natalie turned towards me. "So, Sutton, what are you getting?"

"I don't know, vanilla?" That seemed like the safest choice. You knew exactly what you were getting, and it could be mediocre, but you'd never dislike it.

"You cannot start your summer tasting with vanilla!" She narrowed her eyes at me for a second, then the smile snapped back onto her face. Natalie seemed genetically incapable of being or staying mad. "That's the lamest way to start. At least do rainbow sherbet."

"I like vanilla," I protested. There was no reason to deviate from what I knew I liked.

"I don't care," Natalie shook her head. Her pony-tail started to loosen, and she reached up and tight-ened it. "You have to try every flavor at Brittany's, so you might as well start with the unknown."

"It's a good metaphor for what we're trying to do this summer anyway," Nora said, reaching into a giant bag slung over her shoulder and digging out a five dollar bill. "Do something slightly unexpected, but not unexpected enough to land us in real trouble."

She clearly had not read her own summer bucket list. The gates on our local beach said that the park closed at dusk, and skinny dipping was not allowed. And stealing pants could be considered, well, stealing.

"To be totally honest, I might be in stomach trouble if I eat that ginger guava attempt at ice cream." Natalie pulled the scrunchie out of her hair onto her wrist, inspecting it for a second before sticking her hair back into a ponytail. "This place."

Before I had a chance to redo my ice cream choice, Natalie had already marched up to the counter. "One Cherry Mary, one mint chocolate chip, and one lobsterette."

Somehow I knew that I was going to be the one ending up with the lobsterette. It was pale pink ice cream with chunks of actual lobster in it. It might have been one of the few ice cream flavors weirder than the kale avocado.

"Stick our new friend with the lobsterette. Natalie, Sutton's never going to speak to us again," Nora gingerly took her mint chocolate chip from Natalie, holding it an arms' length away from her. "Actually, I might never speak to you again, either."

"Okay, Sutton," Natalie said, raising her voice so

slightly as Nora started to sniff her ice cream and make gagging noises. "Since Nora's clearly only interested in complaining about perfectly good ice cream, how about you fill me in on your summer plans? Speak loudly so you can drown out all the whining."

"It's disgusting!" Nora sniffed at her ice cream and made a face. "I'm not even being a drama queen!"

"I'll trade," I offered, holding up my faintly pink ice cream with chunks of lobster. Hopefully it was lobster.

"According to my summer bucket list rules, trades for ice cream flavors aren't allowed." Natalie took a giant bite of her cone.

"Says the one who got cherry garcia!" Nora interrupted.

"Ignore the drama queen. Sutton, summer plans."

The words were almost out – I was going to practice for soccer, and work at my internship, and get a head start on my college applications. It was my standard answer, the one I'd given everyone before. But somehow, with lobster ice cream in front of me, it seemed too vanilla. Too normal. "I don't know, honestly."

"That is the best kind of summer," Natalie said,

taking an enormous bite of her ice cream and starting to wander towards the beach.

"I mean, I should be doing stuff to get ready for college," I said. I followed her towards the beach, Nora still making gagging noises behind us.

Natalie shook her head. "What are you actually going to get done this summer that you haven't already? It's one of those things – everyone spends all this time stressing about college and the future, the big scary future, and then they wake up one day and realize it's already the future. That's why I started the bucket list!"

"But isn't that just another way of planning for the future?" I asked, taking a bite of my ice cream. This was weird. Maybe if I thought of it as sweet, frozen lobster bisque I'd get through it.

"Not at all." Natalie took another giant bite of her ice cream. "Because the bucket list is about doing things that no one would expect you to do. It's about doing the kind of stuff that you'll never do if you're always thinking about the future."

"I'm still not eating this," Nora whined from behind us.

"Don't even think about dropping it in the sand," Natalie shook a hand behind her in Nora's general direction. "See, that's the thing. College applications will never be on the summer bucket list, because those are things I'll do anyway. The idea of the summer bucket list is making an anti-list. A list that lets us live in the moment."

Maybe that was true, but it sounded like just more things to add to the list of what I had to do. I had to do my internship and college applications already, so why add more things, even if they were supposed to be fun? Mandatory fun wasn't fun. It just meant more things to do.

"So you're doing the list with us, right?" Natalie asked again as she took another huge bite of ice cream. Mine was starting to melt in my hand. There was something about the idea of lobster inside ice cream that I couldn't get used to. It was wrong. Somewhere in the universe, the ice cream gods were crying.

"Of course Sutton's doing the list with us," Nora said from behind me before I had a chance to respond.

I barely knew Natalie and Nora. I knew what kids at any high school knew about each other. I could tell you that Natalie had worn the same green shirt for a week in middle school, and the middle school mean girls had relentlessly teased her. I could tell you that Nora had been in my kindergarten class and then my AP Bio class, and that she was one of the people you wanted in your study group.

But I didn't really know anything else about them, I realized for the first time. I didn't know anything more than the surface. And that felt somehow like my loss.

"I'm in."

FOUR

"Sutton?" I was sitting at work, renaming files in the proper firm style. Bethany had a very exacting style guide for these things.

"Yes?" I turned over to Bethany, who was standing in the doorway.

"Can we talk about your outfit?" She raised an eyebrow, which was so perfect it had to be plucked.

I glanced down. The temperature had hit ninety outside, and I'd decided that it was smart to wear a sundress to work rather than the heavy wool pants that my mom had given me. The air conditioning was so intense that I was always frozen, leaving me shivering during work and drenched with sweat when I stepped out to eat lunch by myself.

"Yes?" I glanced down again. There were no

stains, nothing to say that the dress wasn't up to professional standards.

"This is a professional office. You need to make sure that you are dressed like it. It would be inappropriate for one of our clients to walk in and see you wearing a bathing suit coverup."

This wasn't a bathing suit cover up. It was a totally normal dress. I swallowed. "I'm – " I was going to defend myself, say that I had worn this dress to plenty of school events last year, and no one had ever complained. But the words escaped me. "I'm sorry. I won't do it again."

"Good." Bethany turned and clicked away, leaving me in the office.

I stared at her for a second, the anger finally coming. I sat in this windowless office all day, where no one could see me, and she was going to be mad that I was wearing something that was totally appropriate? I hadn't come to work wearing a sports bra or anything.

This was what I was spending my summer doing. Sitting in a windowless room, wearing clothes that were supposed to be my winter clothes.

At three-thirty, Bethany left for something, and I decided that it was time to go. I couldn't sit in this air conditioning any more, staring at the wall and renaming files.

I walked back out to my car and opened it to let it cool down, a rush of hundred degree air billowing out as soon as I opened the door.

I stood for a second, letting the car cool, then glanced around the parking lot. It was empty except for a few cars. In the distance, I could hear the sound of the water and the cries of seagulls.

And this was what I was doing. Standing here in a sundress that I'd loved before today, at a job that I didn't care about.

It wasn't quite melancholy, but I was feeling something. It was the sort of sadness I'd always gotten on the afternoon of Christmas day, when the presents had been opened and all that was left was to retreat to my room alone. It was the feeling that things would never be as good as they were in my childhood memories, that summer would never be as full of hope and potential as it once had been.

I leaned my head against the extremely hot top of the car, then slid in and drove.

"SUTTON!" Michael's voice called across the court.

I wasn't quite sure how I'd ended up at the tennis courts. I'd been driving around town, windows down, not ready to go home, but not sure what else there was to do. I'd had the vague sense that other people in this situation would have called their friends, or their significant other, but that wasn't me.

It wasn't like Dylan would have responded either. Lacrosse was his biggest priority right now, and I had to respect that. He was going to be focused on the future, like I should be. Dylan wouldn't have broken the rules at work. He would have worn the perfect outfit for all the clients he could have impressed. He would have probably even networked with them.

But there'd been some kind of draw for me towards the tennis club, like it was the one place where I knew I could find noise and activity, something to distract me.

"I wasn't expecting you to come today," Michael said, leaning forward and brushing away a few strands of hair that were matted to his forehead. "Actually, I wasn't expecting you to come at all."

I was happy he hadn't asked me to explain why I was there. "I know. I don't – I mean, I wasn't expecting to be here, so I didn't bring any of my tennis stuff."

"That's too bad. I was looking forward to playing against you again. You're making me better." He reached for his water bottle and took a drink, his eyes still on me.

"I told you, you don't have to flatter me." I wasn't good. I was nowhere near as good as Bristol was.

"Sutton." Michael fixed me with a steady gaze, his blue eyes seeming even bluer in the sunlight. "I don't believe in flattery."

My stomach lurched forward for a second, but his eyes didn't leave mine. I felt myself suck in my breath, then blurted out, "So what are you doing here? I mean, other than coaching?"

"I was going to clean up some stuff before I go for a run." His hand went back to his forehead as though to brush away some more hair. "It's too damn hot. I thought I was going to do ten miles today, but it's not happening in the heat."

"You run for school, right?" It was one of those facts that I just knew, but I had to ask to be sure.

"Cross country and track. The longer the better." He grinned down at me – he was easily a head taller than I was. "I mean, it's a lot safer than soccer. I don't have to wear a face guard."

"I don't really like soccer." The words were out of my mouth before I could stop them. It was something I'd never told anyone before, because soccer was expected. Everyone had to play a sport to get into college around here. Bristol had already taken lacrosse, so I had to take something different. I didn't go head to head with Bristol, because she always won.

"Then why do you play?" Michael had stopped walking and turned back to face me, his eyes grazing my face.

"Because it's one of those things that you do." Everyone played sports, just like everyone went to college. It was practically part of a life plan. You had to do enough to get into college, and soccer was part of that.

"Who does that?" he asked, rolling his shoulders.

"Everyone!" I swept my arm out towards the imaginary hordes of fellow high school students. "Can you name a single kid in our high school who doesn't?"

"Emily Matson?" He leaned slightly to the right, his head cocking to the side.

"That's because she's an internationally famous violinist." I shook my head. "Bad example."

"But why does the fact that everyone does something mean you have to do it?"

"It doesn't!"

Michael and I stood staring at each other for a second. I could hear his breath, slow and steady. My heartbeat had started to speed up, thudding against my ribs.

He smiled slowly, the corners of his mouth incrementally inching up. "Sutton, I think you just contradicted yourself there."

"I – " Blood rushed to my face and I broke his gaze, staring down at the ground. I could tell that I wasn't going to win this argument. We stood in silence for a few seconds, Michael's gaze over my head, me turning slightly so I didn't have to stare at his chest.

"So," Michael said slowly, breaking the silence. "If you don't have your tennis stuff, want to come on my run with me?"

There were very few things that sounded more miserable than that. "So you can beat me in both tennis and running? No thanks."

Michael Shipman was a bit of a legend around town. Our high school took sports seriously, but we'd never been that good at running, at least until Michael had come back. Sophomore year, he'd led the team to second place in the state, and then last year, while the team had taken fifth, Michael had gone onto nationals.

People hadn't expected it. Michael's dad had been Coach Shipman, the coach in charge of youth lacrosse. He'd been Bristol's hero growing up. He'd been the dad everyone secretly wished they had, and then he'd died of a heart attack at home one gray Wednesday.

I'd gone to the funeral with everyone else. Bristol had broken down and sobbed in the front row, flanked by her friends. I sat in the back next to my dad and watched the proceedings from a distance. Michael had been at the front, and his shoulders had shaken a couple of times as the organ played.

My sharpest memory was of Michael walking up to the podium for the eulogy in a suit that was a little bit too small, bunching up around the shoulders. His voice kept cracking as he tried to deliver the speech, and he had started to cry midway through, his face turning red.

I'd never told him how bad I felt directly. I'd known him, or known of him, all my life, but every time I saw him after the funeral, it seemed to be too late to say anything. Like he'd already recovered, and there was no point in me dredging up the memories of his father. I didn't know how to say sorry without making things worse, so I didn't say anything, and we glided along like nothing had ever been wrong.

"If you promise to lighten up your serve next time we play, I can slow down a bit for you," he said, reaching for a tennis ball to toss.

"A bit? What's your record mile time?" I asked.

Michael started to smile, almost reluctantly. "My mile's not all that great."

"Above or below six minutes?"

Michael's eyebrows shot up. "Below six. Well below six."

His eyes held mine for a second, and I felt myself catch my breath. I forced myself to roll my eyes and look away. "And that's supposed to convince me to come run with you?"

"Sutton, it's not always a race." Michael pushed another piece of hair out of his face and rolled his shoulders. "It's just a little fun run. I'll do three miles with you."

He didn't seem to understand that the words fun and run didn't belong in a sentence together. "That's the longest we ever have to do for soccer, and you're calling that fun?"

"Come on. I promise I won't be a hardo and leave you behind," His hand started to reach towards me then drew back abruptly.

"Can I take you up on that offer some day where it's not ninety degrees?"

Michael laughed, squinting down at me in the sun. "If you're going to give me excuses like that, you should expect me to show up at your house some day when it's twenty and snowing and drag you out."

"Yeah," I replied. "If I ever have time." It wasn't like I was ever free during the school year. I had a demanding course load, and this year was college application year.

"Sutton, you have to make time for the things you love." Michael's eyes were steady into mine again, and I glanced away, down at the court.

"Sure, but there are plenty of things I have to do, so it's not like I can just pick up and go every time I want to do something." Life didn't work like that. You had things that you had to do, and if you didn't do them, they'd catch up with you. I knew that.

"For example," Michael said, as though he hadn't heard me, "what are you doing for yourself this summer?"

"I'm working at an internship at a law firm, and I'm studying for the SATs, and I'm – "

Michael stared down at me, and I gulped. His gaze felt too intense for me. "Sutton Greer, none of that is for yourself."

Of course it was for my future. I was doing all of this for future Sutton. "If I don't do it, I won't get into a good college, and then – "

"Then what?" His eyes were still staring into mine, and my heart rate quickened even more. Probably because of the sun. I was probably dehydrated.

"Then – " I'd disappoint my parents. Something would go terribly wrong for me, like it had with Bristol. "I don't know. But there has to be a reason that everyone is so focused on me getting into college, right?"

If it wasn't going to make me happy some day, what was everyone doing it for?

"Maybe, but I don't know what it is," he said, looking past me towards the courts. Now that he wasn't looking at me, some small part of me missed him looking directly at me.

"So how was camp today?" I asked, trying to cover up the silence. I wasn't good at silences. I lived in them too much to want any more.

"You have no idea what these kids are like, Sutton. They're all over the place. It's a disaster." He shook his head again. "I don't know what your internship is like, but – "

"Not like that." I cut him off before he could say anything more. "It's miserable. I literally just sit in a back room at this lawyer's office. I can't even wear clothes that are normal summer clothes. I have to be there and act like I really care about everything, and it's so boring. I don't know how any adult survives if this is what life is."

Michael's eyebrows lifted, and he tilted his head. "You have strong feelings about this."

"No, it's just – " I stopped, taking a deep breath and looking back up into the sun. It wasn't fair for me to complain about my job. I was lucky enough to have an internship, and it was another of those things that I had to do for college.

"Just what?" Michael asked, taking half a step closer to me. I felt my heart skip a beat even as I forced my eyes away from him.

I couldn't be doing this. I had Dylan. Perfect, stable Dylan. Dylan, who had his priorities right, who knew the statistics on high school relationships as well as I did. He never made my heart skip, but he never made it sink, either.

Dylan, who when I'd texted him earlier, had reminded me that I should remember to wear appropriate clothing. He didn't get it, and I couldn't figure out how to explain it to him. And if Dylan was so perfect for me, why was I so excited to talk to Michael all the time?

My phone buzzed in my pocket, breaking the moment. I looked away from Michael and grabbed my phone. *Hello, is this Sutton? Anyone home right now? Because your sister has decided to not answer her own doorbell.* Then a second text. *It's Mia, btw.*

"I should head out," I said quickly, sliding the phone back into my pocket. "It sounds like I have a visitor at home."

"A visitor?" Michael looked at me, in a way that seemed like he didn't think that I was looking for an excuse to get away. I hated myself for the lies I told by omission.

"My sister's roommate is visiting." I paused for a

second. I couldn't explain it all to someone, the silences at home. I didn't know what was wrong with Bristol, just that things were different.

Michael just waited for me to continue, his eyebrows slightly raised. I swallowed again, my throat suddenly feeling dry. "Bristol tore her ACL. And it's been a lot rougher than I thought it would be. You know, you think that Bristol would just bounce back, because she's always been the person to bounce back."

Michael's eyes met mine for a second, then he looked away towards the back of the court. "You know, I think people thought that about me."

I turned, looking directly at him. "After my dad," he started, "all of a sudden, I wasn't Coach Shipman's kid any more. And that's a kind of mourning, you know? You have to mourn the person that you used to be before you can move on."

But that wasn't Bristol, I wanted to say. We all knew that Bristol was going to get better. She was going to start playing lacrosse again.

But before I could find the words, Michael turned back towards me, his hand resting for a fraction of a second on my shoulder. "I'll take you up on a run some other day, then."

I swallowed, then turned away and walked out of the tennis club back towards my car.

As soon as I walked in the front door, it was clear that something out of the ordinary was going on at my house. There was an entire symphony of pots and pans banging around in the kitchen right now. The house had been invaded by a drumming group with poor rhythm.

"Hello?" I called towards the kitchen. My mother wasn't known for banging anything. She'd installed bumper guards on all the sharp corners in the house when we were toddlers and never taken them off.

"Sutton?" Out of the kitchen came a very tall girl holding up a giant copper pot as though she was about to bash my head in.

"Oh, Mia!" I knew that she was going to be here, but still. It was very different to actually see her standing in my mom's kitchen.

Mia had been Bristol's college roommate. When I'd seen their room over parents' weekend, it had been a study in contrasts – Bristol's neat chevron patterned bedspread and desk tastefully decorated with a few small plants and two family pictures, Mia's half of the room covered in clothes, textbooks, papers, and a few empty water bottles. Mia's life was out there on display for anyone who cared to look closely enough.

My first thought had been that they'd never be

friends. There was no way that Bristol would be close friends with someone who couldn't even be bothered to clean up her space. But I was wrong. Mia had stuck by Bristol through everything.

Right after Bristol had come home, the house phone had started ringing. "Hello?" my mom had answered, clearly a bit surprised that someone was using the house phone.

I'd been able to hear the voice at the other end, loud enough that I had to pay attention. "It's Mia. Is Bristol there?"

"I think she's napping, Mia. She had a very stressful day of physical therapy. Why don't you call her directly and she can call you back when she's awake?"

My mom's diplomatic suggestion had not gone over as well as I had expected. "Mrs. Greer, Bristol is definitely awake. She's not good at napping."

My mom had stared at the phone for a few seconds, then said clearly into the phone, enunciating every word, "Mia, if she's not answering her phone, she must be asleep."

I'd heard the sigh at the other end of the phone line. "Not to be a pain in the butt, but I'm pretty sure Bristol's awake. Would you mind at least checking for me?"

My mom had crept up to Bristol's room with the

phone. I hadn't heard the end of the conversation, but the house phone had stayed in Bristol's room for the next month. And now, Mia had moved from calling to coming.

"Hey, Sutton, how are you?" Mia grinned and pulled me into a hug, holding the pot over my head. "You caught me in the middle of trying to make mac and cheese. Does your family not believe in microwavable food or something? I can't find a box of Kraft mac and cheese, and that is absolutely what I want right now."

"Hi, Mia," I said, eyes still fixed on the giant pot that was hovering over me. I wanted to ask what she was doing here, but couldn't think of a polite way to say it.

But Mia heard the question in my voice without any prompting. "I was worried about Bristol. That girl isn't answering her phone, and I thought she was probably bored and lonely. So I came down here."

The idea of showing up here to help nurse my sister seemed ridiculous. But maybe that was part of the best friend magic that I'd never understood, the idea that you'd drop anything if your friend was in need. "You took time off work for this?"

"I am a lifeguard at the community pool. My job involves making sure kids have waterproof diapers. Trust me, after one poop explosion too many in the kiddie pool, I was glad to get away." She finally lowered the pot from its threatening position over my head.

I nodded. Mia had a habit of saying things where I had no idea how to start a response. It was the opposite of everything I'd learned about conversation from Bristol – keep my sentences short, not say too much about myself, but ask lots of questions. Become the person who listens rather than speaks. Mia had apparently not learned this lesson, because she kept up a steady stream of talk as I followed her back towards the kitchen.

"It's so quiet around here. Has Bristol even left the house?" Mia asked, turning back towards the kitchen.

I shook my head, following her. "She isn't feeling well."

"Yeah, sure." Mia raised her eyebrows. "I made her take a shower. It's not leaving the house that's the problem." Before I asked her to explain, she turned back towards the kitchen. "Now that you're home, want to make the mac and cheese? I know that you don't have the good kind, by which I mean the kind that glows so orange that you know something in there is cancerous. Do you at least have the organic imitation?" Mia opened another cabinet, then looked in it and slammed it shut. "Your family tries way too hard to be healthy, you know that?"

My mom did try to be healthy, but still. "She just worries."

Mia dropped the pot onto the counter. "That was not meant as an insult, Sutton, just an observation. Without neon colored foods, you probably didn't have a childhood."

I had had some neon colored foods, back when I was in preschool. I couldn't tell Mia that, though, because she'd start listing off all the things I'd missed. Like a reverse Natalie and Nora bucket list.

"Anyway, I'm going to get your sister. I leave the food selection up to you." Mia pushed her curls back over her shoulder and bounded up towards Bristol's room.

I was secretly relieved that she was the one facing the stale air of Bristol's room. At least in the kitchen I knew what I was doing. I grabbed bread from the drawer and started up the stove, deciding that fancy grilled cheese was the way to go. Bristol had eaten them every day in high school.

I was half expecting Mia to come down the stairs by herself a few moments later. She'd probably tell me something about how Bristol had been napping, which was evidence that clearly we'd been denied naps in our childhood and were sad deprived adults as a reason. But instead, there were two sets of footsteps, one heavy and one much lighter.

I heard Mia's voice before I saw them. "Also, no offense, Brizzy, but that shirt looks terrible on you. Can we ritually burn it in your firepit later?"

Bristol's voice followed. "Mia, you come to visit, and the first thing you do is insult my clothing?"

It was the first time I'd heard Bristol tell a joke. I held my breath, wanting to vanish, as though my presence in the kitchen would ruin everything. I was a spectator to something too private, like spying on my parents catching each others' eyes and turning away to laugh at a party.

"No, actually, the first thing I did was tell your little sister to make me a sandwich." There was a pause, as though Bristol was deciding whether my name justified turning around, retreating to a place where her family couldn't reach her. But after a moment, Bristol started laughing, and I heard their footsteps again.

I pulled the sandwiches off the stove, where they left a line of charcoal on the pan. I stuck them onto plates, scraping off the few burned pieces, and passed one to Bristol and one to Mia.

"Thanks, Sutton," Bristol said, giving me what could have almost been a smile. I took a breath, waiting for the moment to be ruined. But Bristol picked up her sandwich and took a bite.

"Can't believe that you're on your own this weekend. Did you turn down a trip to Vermont?" Mia asked, taking a giant bite of her sandwich, then looking over at Bristol.

"My parents," Bristol said. Mia nodded, a look that I couldn't read passing between them.

I stared at the two of them, my stomach turning. I'd spent all this time tiptoeing around Bristol, doing whatever I could think of to help her with, and then Mia came and it was all better. That I could try all I wanted, but Bristol didn't want me. She wanted Mia, who'd known her all of six months.

I took my sandwich and walked out of the room, knowing that I was an interloper to whatever would happen next. It wasn't fair of me to be jealous. But still. Mia had just come and

That had always been Bristol's job in the family. She was one who did things right, who made things better and brighter. I'd always been the one behind her, her secondhand glory making me smaller.

But I wasn't strong enough to be that person in front.

I went up into my room, opening the window and climbing out onto the roof. I pulled along a book from my shelf that I'd been meaning to start, deciding to leave the SAT study guide on my desk.

I read two chapters, stretching my legs out. I closed the book for a second, looking around the yard. "Can I come join you?" Mia asked behind me.

I turned around to see Mia starting to climb out the window, her hair taking up half the window. "This is neat," she said, stretching her legs out across the roof and leaning back against the house. "It's so quiet here."

"Is it really that noisy in Boston?" Or at Dartmouth? Neither one seemed like the big city to me.

Mia shook her head. "Where I live, you can hear the trains, sirens, and city lights. It's centering, you know? You always know where you are."

I could see what Mia meant. Sitting here staring at the trees in front of the house in the quiet, it was like I could be anywhere.

I let my breath out and sat my book down, leaning back against the house next to Mia. "I'm happy you're here. It's good."

Mia raised her eyebrows slowly, her eyes fixed on mine. "What do you mean?"

"Bristol just seems different around you. Happier." *Normal* was the word I wanted to use, but I wasn't sure if Mia would be insulted.

"It's not like anyone in this family is doing

anything." Mia fixed me with what was almost a perfect imitation of the Bristol death stare. But we were doing things. Everything we knew how to do.

"I'm trying! We're trying." Maybe I didn't always do things the right way, but you couldn't tell me that I wasn't trying. I was trying too hard, if anything.

"No. I didn't mean you. It's not your fault, because you're seventeen. It's your parents I'm mad at," Mia said, leaning against the house and staring out the yard.

"Bristol barely comes out of her room, and she acts all moody and weird." As soon as I said it, I wanted to take the words back. My family didn't talk about each other that way. Bristol was going through a hard time, and I owed her my support, not complaining about her to her best friend. I wasn't the hurt one here. I didn't have the right to complain.

"Sutton." Mia was staring at me, eyebrows still raised. "Nobody stops talking to their family and their friends because of an ACL tear."

"It's really hard for her, though." The reason was on my lips before Mia could say anything further. I knew this part. "Lacrosse is her life."

"That's what I mean!" Mia slapped her hand on the roof and leaned her head back. "Have you asked Bristol how she feels about lacrosse lately?"

Lately, no, because it would be rubbing it in her

face that she had a torn ACL. But Bristol loved lacrosse. It was like one of those word association games – Bristol, lacrosse. "So if it's not lacrosse, what is wrong with her?" I asked finally.

Mia was silent for a second, drumming her fingers along the roof in a steady beat. She eventually sighed and leaned her head back. "Sutton, you have to ask her yourself. She's my friend, and that means that I don't tell you until she tells me I should."

"It's not like Bristol's going to tell me." Something about the quiet night made me feel braver than normal, as though I was finally able to say what had been simmering in my head. Like since there was no one around to hear me, the words hadn't actually been said, and tomorrow we'd gone on pretending I could have never thought such a thing.

"Maybe if you asked her." The wind stopped, and I could actually hear Mia's breathing.

I didn't want to ask her. Because not that long ago, everything had made sense. I had to follow in Bristol's footsteps and work hard, and my life would make sense.

As much as I hated being in Bristol's shadow sometimes, there was also something comforting about it. Bristol had already laid out the path for me to follow – certain grades, certain classes, certain sports.

I didn't need to question what I was doing, or think about my passions or anything like that. I just had to wake up in the morning and do like my sister did. I could look at her and see that she was happy, so when that sad, nagging feeling came, I could remind myself that I was on the right track.

It didn't matter if sometimes I wanted to go for long drives by myself and just get out of town, get away from everything, go someplace where I was someone different. Bristol was happy, and I could be happy like her too.

But seeing Bristol like this had destroyed all of that. If Bristol had done everything right and wasn't happy, then how was I going to get there?

I stared out at the yard, closing my eyes for a second. Mia looked over at me, then down at my book. "I'll leave you to read, okay? Thanks for the grilled cheese."

I nodded, staring down at my book as she climbed back through the window. Suddenly, without her, the world felt almost too still.

I opened the book and started to read again, the night air cooling around me.

THE NEXT DAY, Mia was still at the house and my parents were still in Vermont visiting their friends. If the pizza boxes and dishes on the counter hadn't clued me in to that fact, the extra noise from Bristol's room would have.

Mia had caught me trying to straighten up the kitchen and winked. "Don't worry, I'll be sure it's all gone before your parents come back. They'll never know."

I suspected that my parents weren't going to come back for a while. My mom probably needed a break from worrying about Bristol, and now that Mia was here, they at least weren't leaving her alone. Plus, Mia seemed to be able to get through to Bristol in a way that none of us could.

"Where are you off to?" Mia asked, leaning against the hallway wall and watching me look for my shoes. She was eating a bowl of cereal, the milk almost sloshing over the sides.

"I'm going to work," I said, stopping in the doorway and bending down to tie my shoes. "I'm working for a lawyer this summer."

"So what do you do exactly?" Mia asked,

"I rename files." The words came out automatically. I should have come up with something better, but instead, I'd blurted out the truth.

Mia almost spit up a bit of her cereal. "And that's why people kill themselves to get into law school? I don't understand adults."

"It looks good for college," I said, standing up. I was already starting to get hot in the dress with pantyhose I was wearing today.

"What a waste of a summer," she said, shaking her head. "You're inside renaming computer files. I can't think of something more boring. I'd rather have poop explosions at the pool."

"Thanks?" I said, my voice inadvertently ending on an up note. " I'll see you tonight, I guess."

"I'm not going anywhere, except maybe to take Bristol to get her hair cut so she stops looking like she's in the eighties," Mia said, lifting the cereal bowl up and slurping the milk at the bottom.

"I heard that!" I heard a yell from the next room. It was Bristol, sounding like she did in my memories. Before I could ruin the moment, I hurried out to my car.

Work was much the same today as the days before. I sat in the air conditioning and felt my skin drying out, staring at a computer screen. Mia's words from the morning before had burrowed into my brain and said what I had started to think about this job.

This was why adults competed to get into law school. So they could rename files. I didn't want a life of renaming files.

It couldn't be that bad, though. Bristol had worked here, and Bristol wouldn't have wasted her time on something that wasn't going to go anywhere. Bristol had goals.

My phone buzzed in my pocket, and I glanced over my shoulder before I dared to draw it out of my pocket. It was a text from Natalie. *What do you think about coming over this afternoon? We're done with the minions at five. My house. Rock Ridge Road.*

It felt less like an invitation and more like an order. *I'm in. Thanks for the invite,* I texted back, tucking the phone under my desk just in case Bethany walked by.

Wow, don't ever thank me like that again. You sound like a robot. Gotta go, someone just ran head-first into a chain link fence. Fifteen seconds later, my phone buzzed with a picture of a kid grinning triumphantly, bleeding from a giant scratch on his head. *I'm never having children. God help me.*

It was uncomfortably humid when I left the office at the end of the day. I immediately felt my legs stick to the pantyhose I'd worn to the office that morning. I took a deep breath and unlocked my car, wishing that I'd brought something to change into. I pulled out of the parking lot, typing in the directions to Natalie's.

I hadn't made it past the first stop sign when I suddenly rolled down the windows. The car air conditioning felt so dry and impersonal. Like I was missing my entire summer, my humid, messy, sweaty summer, spending it all in perfectly manicured spaces with perfect temperature air.

I rolled down the windows and turned up the music ever so slightly, turning onto the main road up to Natalie's and speeding at a whole twenty-seven miles an hour.

Twenty minutes later, I pulled into Natalie's driveway. She lived on the outskirts of town on a quiet cul-de-sac, one of those roads where you passed a giant Children Play Here sign before you even made your first turn.

"You actually came!" Before I even had time to park my car, Natalie was bounding out of her house towards me. I reached down and put on the emergency brake, shutting off the car.

My mom had taught me that you always put on the emergency brake, or as she called it, the parking brake, when you are stopped. It was just in case. Just in case your car started to roll, you had an extra layer of protection. It never hurts to be that extra little bit secure.

Nora came out, following Natalie. "Hey, Sutton," she said, raising her chin in greeting.

"I was pretty convinced that you were going to be one of those people who always ends up having something important to do and weren't going to make it," Natalie said, slamming my car door behind me as I stepped out. "Also, wow. You look like you just came from a funeral or something. You know it's supposed to be summer, right?"

As if it wasn't enough to have Mia at home right now, I also had Natalie. "I just came from work."

"Okay, but so did I. Come inside, I'll get you something summer appropriate to wear," she said, turning back towards the house.

"You should just do what she says," Nora said, watching the two of us and not moving from her spot on the porch hammock. "Otherwise, you'll never hear the end of it."

With that advice, I followed Natalie inside her house. Inside, every surface was covered with African rugs and decorations. A huge carved mask hung on the wall ahead of me, seeming like it was staring straight at me.

"Oh, right. I should have warned you." Natalie grinned at me. "My aunt is married to this absolutely amazing art professor from Angola. He made most of the art in the house. It's so cool, right?"

"It's not what I would have expected." That was an understatement — Natalie's house looked like every other one in the cul-de-sac. From the outside, I would have expected a few giant pictures of her playing sports, maybe a framed family portrait, on the walls.

"That's part of what makes it cool, though," Natalie replied. "There's a whole history and meaning behind each piece of art here. When my aunt and uncle started giving us pieces, they explained the whole history and meaning of each one. It's not just decorative – we have to be respectful of the art and everything it represents, you know?" She shook her head. "It's sometimes hard to explain cultural understanding and appreciation to my six year old brother, but we try."

"That's really cool," I said.

"Yeah. I knew that Charles Huntington the Third was a total loser when he came over and tried to make fun of them. Like, he actually tried to take one of them out of a case and use it as a Halloween costume. What a loser." She started to bound up the stairs, and I followed her, unsure how she could have so much energy after a day spent chasing kids at tennis camp. "I mean, the pants had already told me that he was a loser, but in case we needed any extra evidence."

"Please stop making fun of my poor taste in men," I heard Nora call up the stairs.

"Nope, never!" Natalie yelled back, then

shrugged towards me. "Sorry. You might be deaf now. But it was for a good cause."

I followed her into her room. It at least was exactly what I had expected. The walls had silver spots on them, a partially completed sponge painting. One wall had a huge collage of photos of Natalie and Nora, posing with ice cream at the beach, at the pool, sticking their tongues out.

"I keep saying that I'll finish that," Natalie said, looking over towards the silver sponge painting. She opened her dresser and tossed me a pair of shorts and a t-shirt. I pulled on the t-shirt and wiggled out of my pantyhose, which were embarrassingly soaked through with sweat. Even though there was still air conditioning in Natalie's room, it somehow felt different to be out of my work clothes and into things that felt more like me.

"Natalie, you can't talk about me having poor taste in boys. Remember when we stalked Keith Farren?" Nora asked. She had grabbed three cans of seltzer from the fridge and was leaning in the doorway.

Natalie flopped down on her bed and sighed dramatically. "Sutton, you should know that my life is just a total mess at all times."

"She does it to herself," Nora said, cracking open her can of seltzer.

"Okay, some of it is due to my poor decisions, but also, it's because I don't want to settle for just anyone. I want a love story, Sutton."

"A love story?" I asked. "What does that even mean?"

"Yes. I want a love story. I want the kind of relationship where it's fireworks and fights and explosions and passionate love. I want to know what it's like to feel like you can't live without someone and to be the happiest person in the world when they're around. I don't want to date someone who has all the personality of flat seltzer."

"That's a Charles reference," Nora said under her breath.

"Yes, that was," Natalie said. "But flat seltzer is what I don't want. And so, yeah, sometimes I get into situations where I chase after people too hard, and sometimes I end up breaking my own heart. But it's worth it in the end. I don't want to live in a perfect, controlled world."

"This is the speech that Natalie gives every time I tell her that her life is a mess," Nora said, sitting down on top of Natalie's desk, which was strewn with papers and books. "I've heard it about three thousand times."

"My life is a mess, but I own it," Natalie said proudly, reaching for her seltzer.

"Sutton, are you dating anyone?" Nora asked quickly, cutting Natalie off before she could start talking again.

"Dylan on the lacrosse team," I answered, leaning back against Natalie's dresser. A final drop of sweat ran down my back, and I shivered.

"Is he your great love?" Natalie asked, popping up into a sitting position and cracking open her can.

"He's good," I said automatically. It wasn't a great love story, but it had always worked well enough. Dylan was always there, and I could predict everything that was going to happen with him. "I mean, we have a lot in common because he plays lacrosse and my sister used to play lacrosse."

Natalie and Nora shared a look. "A shared love of lacrosse does not sound like the makings of a truly great love story."

"It's not," I blurted out. I couldn't think of a single conversation that I'd had with Dylan that hadn't gone back to the topic of lacrosse or his training or his classes. It wasn't the kind of passionate love story that Natalie was talking about, where I didn't know how to live without Dylan. With him away at camp, I couldn't remember the last time we'd actually talked. We'd traded a few text messages about our days, but that was it. I wasn't even sure if he knew that Mia was visiting.

It was convenience. It was Natalie's flat seltzer. It was hydrating enough, tasty enough, and even if you shook it up, you wouldn't get bubbles and an explosion.

"But I'm not looking for a great love story," I said finally, after the silence had gone on for just long enough to be awkward. "It's high school. And things with Dylan are easy enough."

"That sounds boring as hell," Natalie said, not sparing words today.

Nora glanced over at me, her eyes traveling my face as though she wanted to make sure that I was okay. But if anything, I was embarrassed of myself, embarrassed to admit I'd gone for flat seltzer. "Ignore Natalie. The single girls here can't judge you."

"We can totally judge. We just might be hypocrites for it," Natalie shook her head. "And honestly, that's my favorite type of judging."

"Well, not to change the topic," Nora said, in a way that left no doubt that she was changing the topic, "but it's still light out, and I'm pretty sure that berry picking was on our list of things for this summer. Sutton, ready to go?"

Now that I was wearing Natalie's clothes, I was. "Let's do it."

FIVE

Saturday morning, I pushed through the doors into the tennis court, dragging my bag behind me. I'd decided to get out early enough to avoid the worst of the heat.

"Hey!" I heard from behind me, and I turned to see Michael coming out of the building.

"Hey," I said, turning back towards him and flushing from the sun.

"I didn't know you were coming out this morning. I'm supposed to play another match, but are you going to be around after that? I'd be down to hit," he said, his eyes not quite meeting mine.

"Oh, yeah!" My voice had shot up an octave, and I swallowed. "That'd be fun."

"Sounds good," Michael said, waving and

starting to walk towards the far courts. "See you soon."

I waved to him and then headed into the club-house, walking towards the locker room with my bag slung over my shoulder.

As I walked down the hall, I glanced over my shoulder and saw a sign plastered to the wall. *Looking to earn extra money this summer? Want to change childrens' lives? Join us as a summer tennis coach! Do something meaningful and have FUN!*

It was the capital letters in the word fun that got me. It was so much fun that you were going to shout about it. As I looked for a second longer, I saw the smaller writing underneath. *Apply at the main office.*

I stared at the poster for a second longer, unsure why I was even considering this. Tennis had always been something that I played with Bristol, something where I wasn't good enough to share my skills with the rest of the world. I wasn't really considering becoming a tennis coach, was I?

In fairness, most of what Natalie and Nora seemed to do was chase kids around the court trying to watch over them, not actually playing tennis. It strangely made the job seem like more fun. Or more properly, FUN.

I started to walk towards the headquarters of the clubhouse without even realizing what I was doing. I obviously couldn't take a job at a tennis camp. I had my internship, which would look much better on my college applications than being a tennis coach.

"Yes?" the woman sitting behind the counter asked as I walked into the main office. "Can I help you with anything?"

"I saw a poster outside looking for instructors for the tennis camp." I could handle factual statements. I wasn't asking for anything, just stating a fact. I saw a poster.

"Oh, thank goodness. When can you start?" Something clattered under the table as the receptionist turned back towards a file cabinet, starting to rummage for something

"I was actually just coming for – " I started to say, but the receptionist had her back turned still. She started talking as though she didn't hear me. "You don't know the trouble we've had getting people to sign up to teach tennis these days. It's all I have to do something that will look good for college and it'll interfere with my plans to study for the PSAT. It's like, haven't kids these days heard of having a job? Or having fun?"

I opened my mouth. Before I could answer, the receptionist slapped down a sheet of paper and a pen in front of me. "Sign here. Can you take the Saturday morning slot? If you want the afternoons too, you can have them." She clapped her hands together. "I can't tell you how happy I am that someone has finally come and decided to take a nice, normal summer job."

I stared down at the paper. I couldn't disappoint someone who was sitting right in front of me, excited to have me do something. I hated disappointing people.

This was a lose-lose situation for anyone with social anxiety. I scrawled my signature on the bottom of the sheet, and the receptionist snatched it back before I could even add the date.

"Oh, I forgot to ask your name," she said as she tucked my signed form away into a drawer. "I'm Mary."

"I'm Sutton," I replied. "Sutton Greer."

"Your last name sounds familiar," Mary said, staring at me for a second. Great. Here came another *oh, you're Bristol's sister, how's she doing, terrible accident.* But she didn't. "I can't quite place it though."

Ten minutes later, I headed out to the courts with a stack of paperwork about tennis camp and my racket. This had to have been the most ridiculous thing that I had done this summer, but somehow, it felt right. I had thought that I'd feel guilty somehow. But even the idea of having to ask my internship to cut down my hours didn't feel that scary right now.

You'll change your mind if Mom finds out, a voice in the back of my head told me. Mom had been sure that this would be the internship that would help me stand out on college applications. But the reality was, there wasn't that much that set me apart from every other girl from the suburbs. I wasn't an Olympian, I couldn't solve complex math problems in my head, I hadn't started a company at the age of fourteen and sold it to Google. I was just me.

"Sutton!" Michael waved and trotted over to me. His hair was slicked back on his forehead with a sheen of sweat. He glanced down at the stack of paper next to my racket and raised his eyebrow. "Did you just sign up to coach?"

I blushed, probably due to the heat and not to Michael. "I guess. It was an impulse decision."

"You don't seem like someone who makes a lot of impulse decisions," Michael replied, taking a slug of his water.

"I'm not," I said, shaking my head. "I'm trying something new."

"I admire that," Michael said, looking at me in a way that made my stomach clench ever so slightly. "And I guess it means that I'll see you around here a bit more."

"Yeah." My brain seemed to have failed me, and my face still felt flushed. I nodded more quickly than I needed to. "Yeah. That'll be good."

"So you want to hit a little bit and practice for all those kids that you're going to have to hit with?"

I took a deep breath and reached for my racket. "This is going to be new for me. I've never played with anyone except for Bristol and you."

"So no better time to start, right?" he said, his eyes still on my face. "Come on."

We walked to the court, and I dropped my bag and stood across the net from him. He hit the first one towards me, and I completely missed it, letting the ball fly off into the back fence. "Sorry," I called, jogging towards the ball. "I wasn't paying attention there."

I reached down for the ball and threw it back to Michael, who caught it with one hand and started to bounce it off the court.

"You know, you don't have to apologize, right?" Michael asked, cocking his head very slightly as he looked at me.

I caught my breath from jogging back and shook my head. "What do you mean?"

"You don't have to apologize for missing the ball. We're just hitting back and forth for fun. It's only a game."

Nothing in my world was ever just a game when it came to sports. I grew up in a family where we collected trophies like some people collected stamps. Bristol won every sport that she'd ever come in contact with, and I'd chosen a sport where I could at least hide behind my team when things went wrong.

"I just – " I looked off towards the side. "You're right. Sorry."

The corner of Michael's mouth lifted in a smile. "You did it again."

"You got me on that one." He hit the ball gently towards me, and I returned it back to him. I took a deep breath, glancing over towards him. "It's weird being here without Bristol," I said, the words rushing out.

I forced myself to focus on the ball and not look up at him. It was easier that way – easier to focus on the thing I could control and not this conversation. I wouldn't have been able to say half of what I'd said if I'd had to look at Michael and see his reaction, see the pity flit across his face as I talked about Bristol.

"I know what you mean. Lacrosse was that thing for my dad, you know?" Michael hit the ball back towards me, and I lunged to reach it before I missed it. It suddenly felt like keeping the volley going was the only thing that would give either of us the confidence to keep talking. "Everyone knew my dad.

Everyone loved my dad. He had his thing, and he was amazing at it. But I never shared it with him."

I hadn't expected that. It was me judging people on their exteriors again, assuming that he'd play because his dad coached. "You really never wanted to play?"

Michael shook his head as he turned and sent the ball back towards me. "Never really. All the focus and overinvestment? No thanks." He exhaled sharply as he hit the ball back towards me. "And everyone made comments. My dad was Coach, so I was going to have to be great. It was like I wasn't allowed to be a mediocre lacrosse player, because that would have been worse than me not playing."

"Is that why you stopped?" I asked, hitting the ball back over the net.

Michael paused, just missing the ball and then grabbing it. "Maybe? I don't know. It just – after my dad wasn't here, it didn't feel right. It had never felt right from the beginning, but I'd forced myself to push through because it's what I thought I was supposed to do."

"It's like you can't be your own person, because you always have to be the person who's already gone ahead of you. Like I'll never stand out at school, because everyone is waiting for me to be Bristol all over again. And I can't be." I'd never be Bristol. I'd never be as smart, as funny, as pretty and successful. I was just me.

"Yeah. Standing in my dad's shadow." Michael reached down and tapped the ball gently across the net, back to me. "That's what my grief counselor used to call it."

"Your grief counselor?" It slipped out before I could stop it. Michael had never been the kind of person who'd I imagined going to therapy – he'd always seemed too quiet to talk about his feelings with anyone, let alone a stranger with a medical degree.

"I started going after everything happened. And it helped." The ball bounced off the court before I could return it, punctuating his statement with a thud. "It's like I didn't know that I was anxious until I started going. All of a sudden, I didn't need to run sixteen miles before bed. I wasn't getting up in the middle of the night to check on my sister and make sure she was still breathing. I was more okay after."

He turned to hit the ball and missed, the ball crashing into a water bottle that someone had left standing on the court. "Sorry," he said softly as we both watched the water form a puddle. Water rushing out, never to be put back.

. . .

THE NEWS that I had taken a job coaching had spread very quickly. As soon as I was done with Michael, Stacey showed up on a mission to give me an official orientation.

"So this," she said, pulling open an old cabinet to reveal a small army's worth of medical supplies, "is the first aid cabinet."

"You have all of that for tennis camp?" Not for the first time, I wondered what I had gotten myself into.

"Parents are annoying." Stacey shut the cabinet, pushing a roll of gauze back in before it could fall out onto the ground. "We have like six kinds of gauze, because the parents last year thought that the gauze we stocked up on wasn't good."

"Isn't it just gauze?" I was pretty sure you could fix most things with just a band-aid. Hopefully, since I didn't know any more first aid than that.

"You would think. But no. Apparently, the gauze that we bought last summer was not made out of organic cotton. And some parents would like you to know that they will not put inorganic cotton gauze on their children's injuries." She rolled her eyes. "Natalie and Nora are lucky that I took the job managing this thing this year."

"That's impressive, managing all of this." I wasn't saying it just to be nice. This felt like one of those jobs that was ten times more work than it looked like from the outside.

"This is going to sound weird, but I like being in charge. I like managing things. I like watching everyone leave at the end of the day looking happy and knowing that I made that happen." She tightened her ponytail. "And also, I didn't think I could deal with another year of managing crying children. I'm never going to be a parent."

As though to prove her point, I heard a scream from the far court. "Nora! He stole my ball again!"

"God bless Nora and Natalie," Stacey muttered under her breath. She looked up suddenly and grinned at me. "That's going to be you next week. Fake more enthusiasm."

"I'm ready for it," I replied. Strangely, it didn't feel all that faked. Fun with capital letters.

"I think I told you everything you need to know," Stacey said as we walked back towards the clubhouse. "Oh yeah, and tell the kids to hydrate. Tell them to hydrate and put on sunscreen so many times that you think you're going to fall asleep saying those things to yourself."

"Why?" I asked as we left the clubhouse. Stacey passed me the water bottle I'd left in the fridge.

"Because if I have a record that you said that thing twenty-seven times, and I have a parent call me hysterical because little Timmy didn't drink enough water and is going to get wrinkles at the tender age of eight, I get to tell that parent to go screw themselves." She took a long slurp of her own water. "In nice words, of course."

"I really don't envy your job," I replied. I couldn't imagine telling an adult to go screw themselves. I apologized when Bethany attacked me about my dress.

"To each their own. I don't envy what you're about to go through." Stacey leaned back against the counter and sighed. "On a totally different note, want to come out tonight? I'm going to hang out with some people at the Orchards tonight if you want to come." The Orchards was a park on the outskirts of town that always had parties that I was never invited to.

"Oh. I'd love to, but – " But what, actually? There was no point going home and sitting alone in my room, or alone in the living room, listening to see if I could hear Bristol and Mia upstairs chatting. Mia probably wouldn't even be home. She'd gotten a job at Starbucks last week, then borrowed Bristol's car, driven up to Boston, and come back with suitcases full of her stuff.

"But what?" Stacey asked.

Nope. I wasn't getting in my head. "But nothing. I'll see you tonight."

I headed home to change and shower. I pulled up to the house and leaned back against the seat for a second, giving myself a moment. Maybe I'd order pizza for everyone tonight. Maybe that would help things.

To my surprise, I could hear noise when I opened the front door. "Hello?" I called, walking through the hallway towards the kitchen. "Bristol?"

"Can't cook to save her life!" I heard Mia's voice call back. I walked into the kitchen, spotting Bristol elbow deep in cookie dough.

"It's part of the recipe!" Bristol said back in the loudest voice I'd heard from her in days. She flicked a piece of cookie dough at Mia, who ducked and avoided it.

"Raisins, Brizzy! No sane person puts raisins in perfectly good cookies and ruins them!" Mia's face looked like she'd seen someone threaten murder. "Were you raised by wolves?"

"Sort of, yeah," Bristol said, taking a large chunk of cookie dough and eating it. "Hi, Sutton."

"Hey," I said quietly. Bristol looked – different. Maybe it was that she was wearing the clothes that I expected to see her wearing, a Dartmouth t-shirt and athletic shorts, her hair done up in a knot. Maybe it was the fact that she finally looked like she was smiling again after everything. She looked like her old self.

"You got here just in time to see Bristol commit a crime against this otherwise excellent cookie dough," Mia replied. "Raisins. I literally cannot believe it."

"You seem to hate every part of my recipe," Bristol replied, scooping out another fingerful of dough.

"First you wanted to cut the sugar in the cookie recipe down, then you wanted to cut the chocolate chips in half, and now you're talking about raisins? What the hell?" Mia asked.

Bristol looked her directly in the face. "You're right," she said, her voice louder than I excepted. "You're right, Mia. Screw that." She reached for a bag of chocolate chips the size of a small baby and dumped them all into the cookie dough. "I'll eat the damn chocolate chips if I want to."

"Hell yeah!" Mia said, high-fiving her.

I stood in silence for a second. I wanted to join in, to tell them that I also didn't like the raisins in cookies. It felt like imitation, pretending to be healthy when at the end of the day, it was a cookie. But this wasn't a conversation where I'd been invited in, so I turned and headed up the stairs instead.

Upstairs, I stared at my closet for a second,

wondering how I'd somehow ended up without any party clothes. I should have at least one outfit that made sense. But no.

I glanced down at my phone. I hadn't spoken to Dylan for the entire week. I should call him while I was getting ready. He was still my boyfriend, after all. *I'm free for a little bit. Call me?* I texted him, and five minutes later, my phone rang.

"I can't talk long, Sutton," I heard Dylan's voice on the other end as he picked up. "I need to go to run extra drills tonight with a few of the guys. We're going to practice before we have a practice scrimmage tomorrow."

"Right. I wouldn't want to stand in the way of your training." The words came out automatically, almost like I was listening to someone else say them. It was extra practice before extra practice? It wasn't like Dylan was going to be a professional athlete.

No, I reminded myself. You like this about him. You like that he's focused on his future. You like that.

"Have you been training for soccer?" Dylan asked, his voice distracted. In the background, I could hear people shouting, calling to him.

"No, I haven't." I should have been. At this rate, I'd be put back onto the junior varsity team, the ultimate insult for a senior who'd played the past three years. But school in the fall seemed so far away. "But

I signed up to work at tennis camp. My first day is next week."

"Tennis?" Dylan's voice was skeptical. "You don't play tennis."

"Not competitively, I don't," I replied. It felt like a ridiculous turn in the conversation. How was I supposed to tell him that in fact, I did play tennis, that I'd always loved playing tennis with Bristol, that it was something about myself that it felt like I was rediscovering this summer?

"That's not very smart if you're trying to optimize your college applications," Dylan said, his voice smug. "Recruiters don't want to see you jumping around all over the place. They want to see a clear passion and development of that passion."

Like you're doing with lacrosse, I thought. "Like I'm doing with lacrosse," Dylan finished for me.

"That's true." He was right. I knew it, but it didn't stick in my mind the way that it once had.

"I've really improved on my form since I've been here," Dylan informed me. I zoned out for the next three minutes, idly going through my closet, making agreeing noises into the phone.

I had completely lost track of where Dylan was in his story when my stomach rumbled. "Hey, Dylan. I'm going to go. I'm going to a party at the Orchards later, and I need to eat dinner first."

"You're going to a party at the Orchards?" Dylan's voice was reproachful. I never went to the Orchards normally. I wasn't the kind of person who'd risk being at a party. It could mess up my college applications if something went wrong.

"Yeah." Stacey had invited me, and now I was going.

"Well, I'm going to go practice with my friends. It's critical that I keep improving my skills so that I have a chance to really impress the recruiters." Dylan's voice had regained its old smugness, its old surety. "Bye, Sutton."

"Bye," I said, hanging up the phone. It clicked off, leaving only static on the other end.

I looked back at my closet. There was a top that I'd bought a year ago, a tank top with ruffles and a bit of a low back. I'd never worn it out before, because it always seemed like too much. But maybe tonight would be a good time.

I changed into my party outfit, grabbing a sweater in case it got cold, and headed downstairs. The entire downstairs smelled like baking chocolate, and as soon as I reached the kitchen, I could see stacks of cookies lying on the counter.

"I was thinking about getting pizza. Does anyone want any?" I shouted.

"Yes! Pizza!" Mia called from the living room.

She and Bristol were crumpled on the couch, a giant pile of cookies sitting in front of them.

"I don't know if I want pizza after all these," Bristol said, gesturing to the cookies.

"Oh come on. You always want pizza. A nice savory treat after all these sweets!" Mia grinned. "Extra cheese, extra meat, and banana peppers."

I raised my eyebrows slightly and glanced towards Bristol. Normally, we got one pepperoni pizza on a regular crust, and one veggie pizza on a cauliflower crust. "Yeah, extra everything sounds good," Bristol said. "But add mushrooms too."

"Mushrooms on pizza and raisins in cookies. You are a strange person. It's a good thing I love you so much," Mia replied, taking another bite of a cookie. "Sutton, you're all dressed up."

"Yeah," I said, glancing down at my outfit. "I'm going to a party tonight."

"A party?" Mia leaned back and examined me again. "This is what the Greer sisters consider a party outfit?"

"Don't make too much fun of my sister. She hangs around my mom a lot." I glanced over at Bristol quickly, but couldn't see her face as she turned back towards the cookies.

"You know, if you drink tonight, you can give me a call, and I'll come pick you up," Mia said, settling back into the couch. "Obviously you're not going to get in trouble with me if you do, although I do reserve the right to make fun of you for the next ten years."

"I'm not planning on drinking," I said quickly. I was going to a party at the Orchards. That was enough for me.

"Right," Mia said. "That's the point. You're not planning on drinking, or you wouldn't have driven there in the first place. I'm just saying, if things transpire differently than you've planned, you can give us a call and we'll come pick you up."

"Speak for yourself. I have no desire to relive a high school party," Bristol said, stuffing a cookie into her mouth.

"I will come pick you up by myself in Bristol's car then." Mia threw a pillow towards Bristol, who caught it effortlessly. "Ruining all my fun, Brizzy."

"You make your own fun," Bristol replied, throwing the pillow back at Mia.

"Oh, shut up." Mia started to laugh. I walked into the kitchen, staring at my reflection in the window. Maybe it wasn't an outfit Mia thought of as a party outfit, but I didn't look like normal Sutton, either.

The doorbell rang, and I opened the front door. "Sutton, right?" the guy at the door asked, holding out pizzas towards me. It took me a minute to recognize him from chemistry the year before.

"Yeah, I am," I said, taking the pizza from his hands and balancing it on my hip. "Marcus, right?"

"Yeah, Marcus." He smiled slightly. "Haven't seen you around this summer. I thought you were off at camp or something."

"No, I just – " I paused. "I haven't been able to get out much."

"That's too bad," Marcus said. "It's been a good summer."

"But I'm going to the party at the Orchards tonight," I blurted out before I could stop myself. "Stacey Chapman invited me."

"Cool, I think I'll see you there," he said, grinning at me. He looked over at the pizza that I was holding. "And also, who orders banana peppers, pineapple, jalapenos, and pears on their pizza?"

"Pears?" I said, taken aback. I must have clicked the wrong thing on the app. I shook my head. "You know. I love pears on my pizza."

"Well, enjoy your pear pizza," Marcus waved to me as he walked back to his car. "See you later."

"Bye," I said, closing the door.

"Pizza's here," I yelled down the hallway, walking towards the living room. I set the pizza down directly on the coffee table, ignoring the voice in the back of my head that reminded me it could leave marks.

"Are these pears?" Mia asked, lifting up a slice and staring at it skeptically, her eyebrows knitting together. "On a pizza?"

"Sorry. I hit the wrong button on the app." I grimaced slightly, hoping she'd accept that as my apology.

"It's still pizza," Mia shrugged, peeling off a piece of pear and sticking it in her mouth. "You can't really ruin pizza."

"You can ruin pizza. If you had my mother's tofu cheese and cauliflower crust pizza, you would fully understand that pizza could be ruined," Bristol replied, pulling the banana peppers off her piece.

"I thought you liked the cauliflower crust pizza," I blurted out. That was why we ate it all the time. Bristol liked pizza, and that was a healthier version.

Bristol was quiet, pressing her lips together and not looking up at me. "Sometimes people pretend to like things to be polite, not because they actually like them," Mia said, more quietly than I expected. "Sometimes people are just lying to be nice."

I looked down at the pizza on the coffee table. The cheese was starting to congeal, the pears wilting. "Yeah," I said. "I'm going to head out to my party. You guys have a good night."

I grabbed my keys and walked out to my car. I drove out to the Orchards. I parked my car on the side of the gravel road that passed for a parking lot, then stepped out into the night. The air was already slightly cold compared to the humidity of the day. Up ahead, I could see a fire burning and hear the people up ahead.

I walked over to the party, glancing around to see if I knew anyone. It looked like thirty or fourty people already standing around, clutching plastic cups.

If this was a party, I could do this. It wasn't what I'd pictured a party to be – there was no one dancing on tables, no one throwing things into the fire, no one even yelling. It was just people hanging out.

"Sutton, you made it," Stacey said, coming up beside me. I jumped slightly, realizing that I'd been lost in thought. "You look great."

"Thanks," I said, pulling my sweater around me. I didn't know if that was true, but I would take the compliment any day.

"Let's get you something to drink," Stacey said, nodding towards the party. She was wearing jeans and a tunic top, a much better outfit. I shivered, feeling entirely overdressed.

She passed me a plastic cup. "Well, cheers," she said, clinking her plastic cup with mine. She took a sip of hers, and I took a sip of mine to mirror her. It was seltzer that tasted just like regular seltzer. "How's the rest of your summer going?"

"My sister's home," I said, the words tripping out. I hadn't told Stacey about Bristol, had I? She probably already knew from the rumors around town that Bristol Greer was home and on crutches. Everyone knew everything in this town.

"Bristol, right?" Stacey asked.

I nodded. Maybe Stacey was the only person who didn't know the story. "Yeah. She's home, and that's not what I expected." I took a deep breath, wondering how much of this was appropriate to tell.

"What do you mean?" Stacey asked, taking another sip of her drink.

I paused. "Her roommate's here. Her roommate from college, I mean." The words failed me suddenly. I couldn't figure out how to say that Bristol seemed normal around Mia again, that I felt useless all of a sudden. That nothing my parents and I had done mattered.

Stacey stood in silence, waiting for me to continue. "I mean, I didn't expect to have an extra person living in my house all summer," I said finally. "And Mia's so different from all Bristol's friends in high school."

"Maybe that's part of going away to college," Stacey said.

"It's more than that," I said. It was how sad Bristol seemed all the time. She didn't want to be here any more. I didn't know her. This wasn't high school Bristol.

"It's my party people!"

Stacey and I looked away from each other to see Natalie walking towards us. Her hair was now streaked with pink. I looked over at Nora, who shrugged in return. "I cannot wait to have a drink and act like I am a normal teenager who does cool normal teenager things, like you'd see in normal teenage movies."

"Sorry, she had a lot of coffee before we came over," Nora said.

"This has been on my bucket list forever. Come to a party, and actually drink something." Natalie shook her head so quickly that I thought her ponytail would hit one of us.

"We weren't expecting to see you here, Sutton," Nora said, turning away from Natalie. Natalie had started scoping the scene, probably looking for the drink to complete the mission.

"I just came to check it out," I said. "I wanted to get out of the house."

"You made it!" I turned to see Marcus, the pizza guy from earlier, wandering over to join our group. "I didn't totally believe you when you said that you were coming to a party."

Maybe I had more of a reputation than I realized at school. "Yeah. I had to see what all the fuss was about."

"Marcus?" I heard the footsteps and turned to see Natalie walking back towards us, clutching not one but two cups.

"Any chance I could get one of those, Natalie?" Marcus asked, turning towards her. He looked at her face, which clearly showed her disapproval at such a demanding ask. "Or not, it was just a reason to talk to you."

Natalie's face turned bright red, and Nora, Stacey, and I all looked at each other. "Has she already been drinking?" Stacey whispered to Nora.

"Oh no. I think you're about to witness what happens when Natalie falls for someone." Nora shook her head. "I was hoping that she'd give it another few days, but nope."

Five minutes later it was apparent that when Natalie fell for someone, she fell hard.

She grabbed Marcus's arm, and everything he said was the funniest thing she'd ever heard. Her laugh echoed around the whole party, and her eyes hadn't left his face for the past five minutes.

"I'm getting out of here before I have to witness

any more of this," Nora muttered, walking off towards the bonfire.

I thought about following her for a second, but stayed with Natalie. Stacey had run off to get another drink, and it looked like she'd gotten waylaid talking to someone on the way back.

I'd stay here and wait for her. Since I'd gotten here,, the party had gotten much fuller. There wasn't anyone who didn't seem fully engaged in a conversation. Everywhere around me seemed like a group of people who'd known each other for years.

I'd known them for years too, but it had always been in passing. Stacey was the closest thing I had to a best friend, I realized. I had plenty of acquaintances – I could name everyone at the party – but no friends. I didn't have someone like Mia, who would drive down from Boston to see me when I was sick and recovering, someone who'd sit in the kitchen with me and make cookies until I felt better.

Dylan wasn't that person, either. Dylan and I always had lots to talk about, as long as we only talked about our respective futures and school and lacrosse. Endless conversations about lacrosse. In my more selfish moments, I wondered if he was dating me because he thought that one day I'd shock him and turn out to be Bristol.

I looked back at Natalie. She was still with

Marcus, looking at him like he was the funniest, greatest person in the world. Her face was lit up, partially from the fire and partially from something else.

I couldn't watch this any longer. I turned and headed towards the beer station, deciding I could get a beer and then find Stacey. I waited at the keg, took my cup, and then started to walk towards Stacey.

I paused. Stacey was now in conversation with people I didn't know. I took a sip of my drink in case that would give me the courage to brave out the awkwardness. I spit it back into the cup almost immediately. It tasted like what I imagined pee would taste like.

I glanced around to see if anyone was looking at me, and when I didn't see anyone, bent down and poured my cup out onto the ground. I could throw the cup behind me into the forest, but that would be littering. I'd just have to take it back to the car and hide it in the glove compartment or something.

I sighed, glanced back at the party, and started walking back towards my car. I had tried, I had to give myself credit for that. If this was school, I at least got partial credit for trying. A participation trophy for not really participating.

"Sutton?"

I looked up to see Michael. He looked even taller

and skinnier in the low light, his arms and legs seeming too large for his body. "I didn't think you normally came to these."

My reputation was preceding me again. "I don't," I said. "Stacey invited me, so I thought that I would come see what it was all about."

Michael walked over towards me and glanced down at the cup in my hand. "Did you finish that?"

I glanced down and took a deep breath before admitting the truth. "No. I didn't want to finish it. But I didn't want to just throw the cup into the woods."

"Not littering. I respect that," Michael said, a corner of his mouth lifting up into a smile. "Are you in a rush to get home?"

That felt like a question with so many ways to answer it. I didn't know where to start. "No," I shook my head more vigorously than was called for in the situation.

"Then pass me that cup," Michael said, reaching towards me and taking the plastic cup out of my hand. He nodded with his head towards the parked cars nearby and walked over to one, tossing the cup into the backseat.

"You don't lock your car?" I asked, walking over towards Michael and checking out the car he'd thrown the cup into. The backseat was covered in gym clothes and empty water bottles.

Michael laughed. "No, but whoever it is, they left their car unlocked. With that amount of mess in the car, I doubt they'll notice an extra cup."

"You're more of a rebel than I expected," I said, the words leaving my mouth before I could hear what I sounded like. That was the sort of thing that Natalie would have said to Marcus, not something I would say.

"I hide it well," Michael said, the same half smile appearing on his face. "Do you want to go for a walk with me?"

I nodded, and followed Michael along the line of parked cars to a small trail. "I found this a few parties ago," he explained, glancing back at me as he started to walk into the darkness. "I'm not good at parties."

"Me neither," I admitted. "I just stand on the outside and watch everyone else there, and I wonder how they have the confidence to just go up to people and start talking."

"I think that too, sometimes," Michael said, taking a giant step over a rock in the middle of the path. "My dad used to tell me that it was all a game, and you just had to think of it like any other game. Your goal is to get people to talk to you, and there are many strategies that can win the game."

"That sounds very coach-like," I said.

Michael laughed slightly. "That was my dad. He had a sports metaphor for everything. I used to make so much fun of him for it, and roll my eyes every time he said one, and now I miss it." He took another two steps ahead, two steps that were easily four of mine, and we reached a clearing up ahead.

"Wow," I breathed out. We were on a hill overlooking the party beneath us. I could hear the voices of the people below if I strained to listen, but they were drowned out by the crickets chirping.

"It was the best thing I've found here," Michael said, sitting down on a rock in the middle of the clearing. He patted the seat next to him. I sat down as well, pulling my sweater around me again. It was chilly away from the fire and the commotion.

"What's it like talking about your dad?" I asked suddenly. I shook my head and looked down at the patch of grass next to my feet, wondering for a second if I could undo the question. "What's it like having one of those points in your life where everything changes, but somehow, time keeps moving on?"

"It sucks," Michael said quietly. He turned towards me, and I could see the reflection of the fire below in his eyes. "There are days where things feel okay again, and then I stop and remember that everything's changed. It's like someone punches me in the stomach. I don't know how to tell people that there are days that are really okay, days where I don't even think about it. There are also days where I hide everything, and I don't even know what I feel any more."

"But it gets better?" I thought of Bristol the first day, hair greasy, wearing the oversized sweatshirt she'd worn for days. The sister I'd never known before, coming home in place of the happy, enthusiastic Bristol I thought I knew.

"Slowly. And it's not a straight line." Michael dug at the ground with his toe, kicking up a tiny clump of dirt. "It's spiky. There are days where I'm much better, and there are still days that I'm not okay. But those days are fewer and fewer, and there are days that I'm happy now, too." He kicked the tiny clump of dirt, and it bounced to the edge of the clearing. "I'm not the same person I was before, but I think that's okay. I'm never going to say that it was for the best, because I don't think anyone can honestly believe that losing your dad is for the best, or that it made me stronger. But it gets better. It gets to be okay again."

We sat in silence for a few seconds. I stared at the piece of dirt, eventually taking a deep breath. "My sister's home for the summer."

Michael said silently next to me, and I didn't turn

to look at him. It was easier to stare at the dirt, to pretend that I was talking to it. "Everyone knew Bristol in high school. She was funny, and outgoing, and she always winning. Bristol was who everyone wanted to be."

I swallowed and forced myself to keep going. "The Bristol who went off to college and the Bristol who came back are different people. I don't recognize her any more. It's like there are two parts of my life, the part where I had a big sister and the part where I don't." I couldn't bring myself to look up at Michael, so I threw my head back and stared directly at the stars above us, blinking to try to keep back a tear. "I feel so stupid talking about this. It's not like for you, where you actually lost your dad. Bristol is still here, but it's like I don't know her any more."

I closed my eyes. I couldn't cry, not in front of Michael, not when he'd gone through so much more than I had. "Hey," I heard him say softly, and felt the pressure of his hand on my knee. "Sutton. It's okay."

For some reason, that was all it took for me to start crying. Not the billions of conversations where I'd felt like I was lying, not the days where we'd all pretended that Bristol was okay, not even the feeling of emptiness I'd had after hanging up with Dylan. It was someone finally telling me that everything was okay.

Michael reached an arm behind me, and I stuck my face in his shoulder for a second, taking a few deep breaths. I shut my eyes, trying to stop the tears, then sat up. "Sorry. I think I ruined your shirt," I said quickly, and Michael pulled his arm out from behind me.

"That's okay," Michael replied. "In the big picture, that seems pretty fixable."

My chest felt like it was actually expanding now that I was finally talking about all of this, letting it all out. "I just don't understand what's going on with Bristol now, and the problem is that we won't talk about it. We're all busy pretending things are fine, and it's not working."

"Have you talked to her at all?" Michael asked, his voice low.

I shook my head. "I don't even know where to start. I know that it's not about her leg. There's something else going on, and she won't talk to me about it. She'll only talk to her roommate from college, and it's terrible that I'm jealous of Mia, but I am."

Michael put a hand behind himself and leaned back slightly. "When my dad died, my sister handled it really differently than I did. She handled it like people expected her to. She cried a lot and talked about her feelings with people." He rolled his shoulder. "I didn't know how to talk about things. She did.

And so everyone assumed that I wasn't grieving, when I actually was."

"But that's different." I shivered a bit and pulled my sweater around me again. "You were both going through a bad situation."

"But it's just as hard for people on the outside sometimes," Michael replied. "I think you and Bristol might just be grieving the past?"

"Maybe. But I just wish that I could say what's wrong." If I couldn't tell Michael what was wrong, it was probably because nothing was wrong. I was probably overreacting to change.

"Are you okay?" Michael asked suddenly, gesturing down at my legs. "I mean, just in terms of temperature. You look like you're cold."

I glanced down at my legs, realizing suddenly that they were covered in goosebumps. Away from the fire, things were a little bit chilly. I hadn't noticed how long we'd been out. "I'm okay. Maybe I should head back to my car and head back. This is probably my sign that I've been out too long."

"I'll walk back with you," Michael said, pushing himself up off the ground and standing up beside me. He rubbed his hands together, shaking off the dirt that had accumulated. "It's probably time for me to call it a night, too."

We walked back down the hill in silence. I could

hear Michael's steady breath behind me as I navigated the path back towards the parked cars, trying not to slip on any of the rocks.

We reached the cars, and I glanced back to see him standing behind me. "Thanks," I said softly. The word felt inadequate and wrong somehow, like there was supposed to be a bigger declaration that I could make. "I'm glad we talked."

"You can talk to me any time," Michael said, stuffing his hands back in his pockets. "I've been there. Good night, Sutton."

"Night," I said, glancing back over my shoulder as I walked back towards my car and got in. I looked back as I pulled my car out of its parking spot, looking back and seeing Michael still standing there, hands in his pockets.

I glanced down at my phone, where I had a text from Stacey asking where I was, then one letting me know that she was sure that Marucs and Natalie were going to start making out at the party. I sighed and shut the front screen of my phone off. Tonight felt longer than the few hours I'd been away from the house.

I drove back home from the Orchards, my headlights illuminating the dirt road and then the houses alongside the path back. I loved driving at night in the summer, where there were no other cars on the road and it was just me and the silence. Nothing to think about, nothing to talk about, just the road ahead of me.

I pulled back into my driveway and shut the car off, heading inside. I walked towards the kitchen. I could use some pizza after being out for so long. I turned into the kitchen and saw Mia sitting at the counter.

"Hey," I said, opening the fridge and pulling out a cold slice of the pear pizza.

"How was the party?" Mia asked, glancing up from her computer. She shut the top, looking directly at me.

"It was good." I sat down at the stool across from her as I waited for the pizza to warm up in the microwave.

"What'd you end up doing?" Mia grabbed the tea mug next to her with both hands and took a sip.

I was about to come up with some ridiculous party story that made me seem much less lame than I'd actually been. That was what she was expecting from someone who went out to a party. But Mia had figured out who I was. "I talked to a couple of my friends. Nothing exciting. I left before things really got going."

"There's nothing wrong with that," Mia said, shutting her computer screen and taking another drink of her tea. The microwave dinged, and I pulled out my pizza slice. "Not everyone is a life of the party person, and not everyone needs to be."

"I'm just awkward." As though to reinforce that fact, I tore off my pizza crust and began to eat it before the rest of the slice.

"Anyone who thinks they're not awkward is, and most people who think they are aren't." Mia shook her head. "I'm awkward."

"You're definitely not awkward." Mia brought the party with her. She always seemed to have a comeback, always seemed ready for verbal sparring. People gravitated towards her, even Bristol. She was my opposite.

"Well, thanks. But I feel out of place all the time. You don't think that I feel out of place here?" She gestured around to the giant kitchen, the stainless steel appliances glinting. "I'm a first gen at Dartmouth. I feel out of place at school, and it's even worse here."

I paused. I hadn't thought about it, actually. It hadn't occurred to me that Mia would feel out of place here, that people would look at her any differently than they looked at me. I took a deep breath. "No, I didn't think about that, and I'm sorry about it."

"The worst kind of people are the people who think that they're really forgiving and really woke, but then when they see someone who doesn't fit in their bubble, they don't know what to do." Mia shook her head. "I miss home all the time."

I sat in silence, feeling worse and worse as the minutes ticked by. Mia was right, and I hadn't noticed. I hadn't thought about what a sacrifice it was for her to be here with Bristol and not at home. I had missed everything.

I opened my mouth, then stopped, not knowing what the appropriate words to say were. Apologizing felt insincere, somehow, like I was apologizing to prove that I wasn't one of those people, to prove that I was the good guy.

Mia snorted. "I thought I was going to hate Bristol when I first met her." I looked over at her. That couldn't be possible. Everyone loved Bristol.

"I got to campus early," Mia continued. "I walk into my dorm room, and I find out that I'm sharing it with a lacrosse recruit from Connecticut. Her name is *Bristol Greer*. Then I saw all the stuff that your mom was moving into the room, matching bedspreads and everything, and I was literally going to ask for a reassignment from the housing office."

"My mom was a lot?" I asked. I could see that. My mom had taken everything about Bristol going to college very seriously.

"Not just your mom." Mia looked over at me. "I

know you live in this town, which is a weird bubble, so you might not see this. But your sister is a walking stereotype. And it took a little bit in college before she realized it and stopped being quite so obnoxious. I still have to call her out on things sometimes. But she's learned a whole lot."

Mia took another sip of her tea and then put it down on the counter. "But you know what? Both of us decided to ignore the stereotype of each other. We ended up as friends anyway. I would do anything for her. She'd do anything for me." Mia shook her head. "I don't want to be here, but she's my friend, and I'm going to be here and stick with her until she's through this. God only knows that your parents aren't doing shit."

That seemed harsh, but my parents were doing what they could. I didn't know how to tell Mia about all the days before she'd arrived, how my mom had prowled outside Bristol's room, hoping to understand what was going on. I couldn't explain the devastation on my dad's face when we'd gotten the first call, the way my parents had immediately sprung into action. They cared.

"She's doing a lot better," I said. Whatever Mia had done had helped. "She almost seems like her old self."

"I wouldn't want her to be like her old self," Mia replied.

"What do you mean?" When I thought of Bristol, I thought of her in high school running through the house, grabbing her things for lacrosse, on the phone with someone gossiping about something.

"People change, and that's a good thing," Mia said, taking another drink of her tea. "You shouldn't be your old self all the time."

That was true, I guessed. I was the Sutton who was coaching tennis camp now, the Sutton who'd gone to a party tonight. "Do you really believe that?" I asked.

She nodded. "I'm like two years older than you are, but I can tell you that nobody knows who they are at sixteen or seventeen. That's totally okay."

I stared out the window for a second, setting the rest of the pizza on the counter. Maybe I wasn't supposed to have all the answers. Maybe that was okay. Maybe Bristol hadn't had all the answers either.

"But," Mia said, snapping me out of my thoughts, "I can tell you that pears on pizza is something that you should grow out of."

I snorted, heading back for my second piece. "Yeah. I agree with that."

SIX

I tightened my ponytail, checking myself in the mirror again. I was ready for this. I could do this.

It was my first day of teaching tennis camp. Outside, I could hear the murmur of kids starting to arrive. "Remember to hydrate!" I heard one of the adults yelling after a kid.

"Are you ready?" Stacey asked, peering her head around the door.

"As ready as I'll ever be," I replied, picking up my racket. Stacey high fived me as we walked out.

"No pulling hair!" I heard Nora yell from a distance. I forced myself not to wince. Maybe this was going to be harder than I expected.

Stacey walked over to the kids, a clipboard held out in front of her like armor. "Hello, tennis campers! I have exciting news for you on this beautiful day!"

The kids seemed to be much less enthusiastic than Stacey was, but they stopped hitting each other for long enough to look up at me expectantly. One of them dropped a racket onto the ground for emphasis.

"Coach Sutton will be your new coach for the summer, and I can tell you that she's great!" That seemed like a bit of an exaggeration, but I'd take any praise that I could get. Stacey started calling names out, and a few kids started reluctantly walking towards me.

"Hi there! So excited to meet you!" I said, bending down to shake hands with the kids.

"Don't do that," Natalie whispered from behind me. "They hate it. The first time I tried it, I got smacked in the head with a racket for my trouble."

Okay then. I stood back up, clapping my hands together. "So who's ready to play some tennis?"

Two hours later, I was ready to collapse onto the court. Time here seemed to fly by faster than at my internship, even though I didn't know what was going on at any individual minute. I had one girl hit by a ball, and I had to promise to braid her hair to get her to stop crying. I'd reminded the kids to hydrate eighteen times, as Stacey had instructed. For that effort, I'd gotten kids pouring ice cold water on each other and shrieking.

"Bye! See you soon!" I called, waving as the kids were walked out by their various parents.

"You survived," Nora said, walking over to me. Her hair was done up in a high bun, and she seemed like she was barely sweating. On the other hand, my ponytail had fallen out, and I could feel clumps of hair stuck to my face with sweat.

"That was a lot." I was going to be so sore tomorrow. My legs were already shaking.

"I bet you're going to quit and go back to that cushy air-conditioned internship now, aren't you? Don't worry, absolutely none of us will blame you." Nora shook her head and took a huge drink of her water bottle.

"This is more fun," I replied.

Bethany had not been too pleased when I told her I'd changed my hours. I'd claimed that it was for tutoring and soccer practice, and I'd gotten a short speech about how Bristol would have "managed her calendar better", but that had been it. Claiming that I needed to do something for college was the magic formula.

"The hair was a huge success. Huge success," Natalie announced dramatically, strutting over towards us. "Nora, everything you said was absolutely, a hundred percent wrong. The kids loved it."

"I didn't say that the six year olds you teach

tennis to would hate it. I said that people with taste and style would hate it," Nora replied.

"Charles Huntington the Third would hate it, wouldn't he?" Natalie asked, fluffing up her hair at the end. Despite being outside sweating for hours, her hair was also magically still in place. "All the more reason for me to love it."

"It seemed like Marcus loved it last weekend," I blurted out before I could stop myself.

"Wait, hold on. Is that Sutton Greer giving someone sass?" Nora asked, turning towards me. "We didn't know you had it in you."

I didn't either. Natalie sighed, clearly deciding to ignore Nora's comment in favor of talking about Marcus. "He's fantastic. He's just great. I can't believe that we've had so many classes together and I've never even noticed him."

"Probably because you were madly fawning over someone else at the time," Nora replied.

"We've gone over this. I don't madly fawn over people. I fall in love, and then sadly, sometimes I fall out of love. It's a natural part of life, which you would understand if you weren't so focused on boys like – "

"Charles Huntington the Third," all three of us at the same time.

"Please tell me we're not talking about that loser,"

Stacey said, walking over. "I will actually throw up if I hear any more about that guy and his awful pants."

"Has this been the only topic of conversation here?" I asked.

"Natalie has shared with everyone how much she hates his guts," Stacey said. "She's had some pretty good burns, actually."

"I don't need to make fun of him. He does it for me when he wears those pants. Or talks, honestly. He should try not to talk if he doesn't want people to make fun of him," Natalie said, shoving her racket into a bag.

"That's not very nice, Natalie." Nora narrowed her eyes at Natalie.

"Sutton, do you want to come get ice cream with us?" Stacey asked. "Celebrate surviving your first day of camp and bribe you into staying for longer?"

That sounded amazing and exactly like what I needed, but not tonight. "My parents are back from Vermont today. I have to be home and get dinner with the family."

"It's my treat next time, then," Stacey said, clapping me on the shoulder. "Thank god we have another coach for this program. It was a nightmare trying to corral all of those kids before."

"Text you later," Natalie called over her shoulder

as I walked back towards the parking lot. At least, I was pretty sure that she was talking to me.

I drove home, keeping the windows down so that the entire car didn't smell like sweat tomorrow. My mom's car was parked in front of the garage, a sign that she was definitely home. I pushed open the front door and walked in, almost shivering as the first blast of air conditioning hit me.

"Sutton?" I heard my mom's voice from the kitchen, and I walked in to see her sitting at the counter. Her posture was much better than Mia's, I noticed suddenly. Stick straight and perfectly poised. "Where have you been?"

"I've been coaching," I replied, reaching into the fruit bowl on the center of the counter and grabbing an apple. I hadn't realized how hungry I was after running around for the afternoon. "It was my first day with the tennis program."

"Your first day doing what?" my mother asked, her eyebrows shooting up. "You're involved with a tennis program?"

"Yeah. I'm coaching kids. I mean, not really coaching, mostly just hitting around with them and getting them excited about the sport," I said, reaching for an apple and taking a bite. I was starving.

"And you're taking time away from your internship to do this?" My mom's eyebrows were still raised.

"I asked at the internship, and I'm going to make up my work at night and skip my lunch breaks." Not that I had any meaningful work to make up, honestly. I could finish a day's worth of scanning in forty-five minutes, so this was actually going to be much better all around.

"I really don't think this is a smart idea, Sutton." My mom's mouth had narrowed into a thin line. "It's very unprofessional for you to ask for a schedule change at your internship, and I don't think you can ask them for a recommendation for college now. And on top of that, you really need to be focusing on getting ready for the school year again. I just don't see how you're going to fit studying for your SATs, soccer, and your internship into this summer."

For a few moments, I'd forgotten about soccer. Practice would be starting up again in a few weeks. The thought of running around the field, the endless drills, the games during the school year, made my heart sink.

But I'd worry about that later. That wasn't an argument that I was going to have with my mom now. "I want to work at a tennis camp, Mom. It's fun."

"Sutton, you have to remember that things aren't always about fun. Soccer can be your source of fun, but we also have to make sure that you're well posi-tioned to get into college. If you don't get into college, fun will be much more difficult for the rest of your life."

I stopped myself before I let out a sigh. "Yeah, I know. Don't worry. I have it all under control."

I'd regret it later if I didn't get out of here. I'd let it slip that I wanted to quit soccer and the internship was a waste of time. I marched up to my room, shutting the door more firmly behind me.

Had my parents always been this uptight? Maybe I'd never noticed because I'd always agreed with them before. Yes, the internship might not be the most exciting, but it was important for my future. Maybe I don't like soccer now, but if I committed and practiced, then things would get better and I'd like it more.

My phone vibrated with a text from Michael – *do you want to come get ice cream with me?*

I looked at the ceiling. I had skipped hanging out with Stacey, Natalie, and Nora for family time. But if family time was going to be just berating me for things, I wasn't sticking around for it.

I texted Michael back – *yeah! On my way, be there in fifteen!* I swung my legs off the side of the bed, and stood up. I walked down the stars towards the kitchen, then took the back door out. Just one less question to have to answer.

I reached Brittany's twelve minutes later, snagging a parking spot on the main street. I jumped out of the car and heard my name called from behind me. I turned around to see Michael waving from his car. "I had my eyes on that spot!" he called, waving at me.

"Not my fault. They're first come, first served," I called back. I started to blush, strangely, because I hadn't done anything wrong.

"I'll see you in a few minutes. I'm going to have to find a new spot now," he called back.

I walked over to Brittany's and waited on a bench outside, looking at everyone with their ice cream. At some point, that had been me.

I blinked again. It had been me back in middle school, but it was me again, just with Stacey and Natalie and Nora now. When I looked at people on the beach, I didn't have to wonder what it was like to be them. I could be them. I was them already.

"Sorry about that," Michael said, jogging up to me. "You know, I was almost on time, but then someone took my spot right out from in front of me."

"I heard that someone was too late getting to the spot, and the earlier person took it," I replied. "Seems like you should practice being more on time."

"Or you should practice sharing parking spots better," he replied.

"Never." And it had even been a large enough spot that I'd been able to parallel park in it, which was a miracle. I'd barely passed my driving test because of that stupid section.

"So what flavor are you getting?" Michael asked as we walked into the ice cream line. "My sister told me they had kale avocado today, which doesn't belong in ice cream."

"Maybe kale avocado wouldn't be that bad," I offered. "It's like a green smoothie, but in ice cream form. That could actually be okay."

Michael shook his head. "No. I'm an ice cream purist. You should not put things into ice cream that don't belong in ice cream."

"So I take it, you've never tried the lobster one?"

"They have lobster ice cream?" Michael's mouth dropped open. "Okay, that's even worse. How is this place still in business?"

The woman in front of us in line gave us a nasty look. I bit back a smile. "So what are your feelings on mint chocolate chips then?" I asked.

"When I said I was an ice cream purist, I meant it," Michael replied. "There should be nothing in ice cream that is a chunk of anything. No cookie dough, no chocolate chips, no nothing. If I wanted to eat chocolate chips, I'd have cookies."

"Rainbow sherbet?" I pushed.

"I'm not sure you're quite grasping this, Sutton," Michael said, the corner of his mouth twisting up into a smile. "Ice cream should be a single flavor, single color, and single texture."

"Which doesn't rule out kale avocado by those rules," I pointed out.

"It does! Kale and avocado are two separate flavors. That violates the single flavor rule, and also, vegetables are not an acceptable ice cream flavor."

I glanced back up at the menu. "What about the cashew cream earl gray?"

Michael sighed. "Another rule. No low fat ice cream, no dairy-free or sugar-free ice cream. If I wanted to eat something healthy, I'd go eat something healthy. This is ice cream. Let's not screw around with it, please."

The woman in front of us sighed again very loudly, and Michael grimaced. "I just hate people who shame other people for eating what they want. If you want ice cream, have ice cream!"

"Unless it doesn't follow your multiple ice cream rules?" I asked, raising an eyebrow.

Michael grinned, his eyes meeting mine. "I didn't say you couldn't enjoy the kale avocado frozen dessert, Sutton. I just said you couldn't call it ice cream."

We'd finally reached the front of the line, and I elbowed Michael. "So after that rant, what are you getting?"

Michael sighed and stared at the menu. "Vanilla. Going with vanilla. Which is about the only flavor I ever like here."

I glanced at the menu. I looked at moose tracks for a while, then shook my head. "You know what, I think I'm going to skip the cinnamon marshmallow swirl today and go for pear and blue cheese."

Michael's mouth dropped. "No. You cannot be serious."

"Watch me," I mouthed back, and stepped up to the counter. "Hi! Can I get one scoop of pear and blue cheese and one scoop of corn on the cob in a waffle cone, please?"

After we'd paid and wandered outside towards the beach, I caught Michael staring at my ice cream. "It looks less disgusting than I'd imagined," he said, tilting his head slightly and staring at my ice cream cone.

I took another lick of the pear and blue cheese. "It's not the best flavor I've ever gotten, but it's not the worst." I took out my phone and snapped a picture, texting it to the group thread I'd recently been added to.

"Do you normally go for the weirdest flavor of the day?" he asked, peering at the visible bits of blue cheese in my ice cream.

I laughed. "No. Natalie and Nora have this summer bucket list, and I got dragged into it somehow." I took another lick of corn on the cob, which was actually pretty good. Not what I would have expected for ice cream, but it somehow felt like summer. "One of the challenges is to try every ice cream flavor here, including the weird ones. I definitely wouldn't have gone for this otherwise."

"How do you know those two?" Michael asked. We sat down on a bench by the water, a couple of seagulls swooping over us and clearly checking out if our ice cream was up for the taking.

"I went to play tennis one day, and it was right as camp was ending," I said, taking another bite of my ice cream before it could be snatched by a marauding seagull. "We just started talking, I guess."

"They're pretty cool," Michael said, taking a bite of his much less interesting vanilla ice cream. "Natalie is one of those people who knows how to make the most boring stuff fun."

"I wish I was as loud as she was sometimes," I blurted out. "I can't imagine dying my hair pink. For starters, my parents would get mad, and then after that, imagine if it didn't look good and I was stuck with a giant pink head for weeks."

Michael leaned back and looked at me. I could feel his eyes on my face and blushed, deeper than I intended. "You'd look good with pink hair."

"You really think so?" I asked, blinking rapidly.

He reached out and brushed a piece of not-pink hair away from my face. "I think you'd look great with any hair color. You'd be one of those people who could actually pull off purple hair if you wanted to."

My stomach flipped, and I wanted to look away. "My mom would probably die if I came home with purple hair."

"Then you should do it. Assuming that you mean die in the metaphorical sense," Michael added. "If the only thing holding you back from something is worrying about your parents, you should try it. Generally, I think parents end up coming around to things more quickly than you'd expect."

"You don't know my mom," I said. He really didn't if he thought that. "She got so mad because I changed my hours at my internship. I got a whole lecture about how my sister wouldn't have done it, and how I should have known that it was going to make it harder to get a recommendation for college."

Michael leaned back. "It's not like college is the only thing that you should be thinking about."

"I know, but tell that to my mom. She's petrified that if I don't do everything right this summer, then I'm not going to get into a good college, then I'm going to end up with a job I hate and never be happy again in my life. So I have to do everything right now, or I'm going to end up screwing myself over in the long run," I said.

"That's just not true." Michael shook his head vigorously, a few pieces of hair flying around his face. "There are so many more important things in life than getting into college, and so many more things that will make you happy than getting a good job or good grades or some stupid sports trophy."

"But that's what everyone seems to want," I replied. "When I look around, it's all people who have good jobs and went to good colleges and played sports. And it's like I don't know what I want if it's not that, you know?"

Michael nodded, and I took another deep breath, followed by a bite of corn on the cob ice cream. I pushed a little of my pear and blue cheese ice cream onto the ground, where I was sure a seagull would swoop down and snatch it. "I think about it a lot with Bristol," I said. "She did everything right in high school, got into a good school, and now she's at home again. I just don't want that to happen to me." I took a huge bite of my ice cream. "She should be happy, you know? Maybe she can't play lacrosse for another few months, but she has everything else she could want. I just look at her and I wonder how I'm supposed to be happy when she's not, you know?"

"I don't think that you being happy has anything to do with Bristol being happy," Michael said. "And do you think that those are the things that are going to make you happy? Just getting into college?"

It would be great if I knew that answer. "But what's supposed to make me happy, then? It's always been doing what Bristol did, or what my parents recommended that I do. I've always known what to do next, and this is like the first summer where I don't have a plan."

"You have plans," Michael said, shaking his head. "You're doing a bucket list with Natalie and Nora. Isn't that a plan?"

"Yeah, but I can't really write 'I dyed my hair purple and stole Charles Huntington the Third's pants on my college applications.'"

Michael's eyebrows shot up. "Why are you stealing someone's pants?"

"Yeah, forget that I told you that," I said, taking a bite of my ice cream. "Nora will kill me if it gets out."

"That is even more reason to explain to me what

is going on," Michael replied. "Why are you stealing someone's pants?"

"It's Nora's ex-boyfriend, and Natalie hates him. Really, passionately hates him. I honestly don't know what he could have done to give Natalie such strong feelings about it."

"I can kind of guess from the name," Michael said, finishing the last part of his ice cream cone. "He seems like he might take himself very seriously."

"He really loves ugly pants. He loves them in a way that would make a normal person want to throw up," I explained. "He has pants with sailboats embroidered on them."

"Fascinating." Michael shook his head. "You know I'm going to need to hear the rest of this pants story at some point."

I winced. "You'll have to protect me from Nora's wrath if I do that."

Michael grinned. "I'm willing to take that chance. I'm pretty sure that I can outrun them if it comes to it. Or I'll distract them with ice cream."

"You mean frozen dairy dessert?"

"Yeah. That's what I meant. Substandard frozen dairy dessert that they will insist on calling ice cream anyway." Michael elbowed me in the side, and we made eye contact for a second too long. My stomach constricted, and I took a deep breath.

My phone buzzed, and I glanced down at it. It was Mia – *Come home, your parents have dinner ready, and I have to head out to my shift.*

I didn't want to go home. The last thing I wanted was to go do family things when I could be sitting here with Michael, eating frozen dairy dessert.

"Who was that?" Michael asked as I tucked my phone back in my pocket and stood up.

"Mia," I replied. "She's waiting for me to come home so she can head over to Starbucks and get away from my parents."

"Does she really need coffee?" Michael asked, raising an eyebrow as I stood up and wiped crumbs and sand off my pants.

"No, she works there. She got a job working at the Starbucks downtown," I said.

"Well, if I ever go get coffee there, I'll have to say hi to her and tell her that you say very nice things about her behind her back," Michael said, giving me the tiniest hint of a grin. My chest constricted.

"She'll have some super witty comeback to that, don't worry," I replied. "Thanks for inviting me out. This was fun."

"Anytime you need a partner to get frozen dairy desserts with, you let me know," Michael replied, giving me a fist bump before I headed back to my car. "See you around, Sutton."

I walked back to the car and drove home. Something was happening with Michael. I didn't know what it was, but there was something going on there. My stomach flipped thinking about it again.

I had to think about something else. I couldn't let myself get into my own head.

I checked my phone in case there was a text or something from Dylan. Nothing.

It didn't help that this was going to be an awkward dinner, I could just feel it. Bristol hadn't had a full dinner with my parents since they'd gotten home, and Mia wasn't there to make things more bearable. In the best case, this was going to be sitting in silence and admiring whatever my mom had picked up from the store.

I parked the car and headed inside. God, I didn't want to do this tonight. I wanted to still be with Michael.

I walked into the kitchen and saw Mom setting up plates on the back patio, so I pushed open the door and went outside. "Sutton, where have you been?" she asked, barely looking up at me as she straightened a fork next to a plate.

"I went to get ice cream with a friend," I replied, holding onto the back of the chair in front of me.

"Before dinner?" My mom's voice had the tiniest trace of disappointment in it, but it was enough to make my stomach clench. Of course it was this on top of my internship.

I took a deep breath. This was not a big deal. In the scheme of things, this was nothing. "I hope you haven't ruined your appetite for dinner with a lot of sugar," my mom continued. "We bought all of your and Bristol's favorites."

"Thanks, Mom." I wasn't even sure what my favorite was supposed to be. Celebratory dinners in this house were always Bristol's favorites, never mine. "But I'm sure I have enough room leftover for dinner."

"Soccer training would do that," my mom said, smiling slightly and standing up straight. I nodded and pressed my lips together.

Bristol came downstairs in an old t-shirt and shorts. "Bristol!" my mom exclaimed. "We got all of your favorites tonight. We're excited to have family dinner."

Bristol tightened her mouth into a thin line and sat down at the table, thunking herself into a chair. I sat down next to her and glanced over. Bristol didn't meet my eyes. We sat in silence, waiting for my parents to come in.

A few moments later, my parents came out carrying a tray of hamburgers and grilled vegetables. "It's great to have dinner on the patio with both you girls again," my dad said. "A nice family dinner for us all to catch up and spend some quality time together." He unfolded the paper napkin that my mom had left on his plate, setting it neatly onto his lap.

"Sure," I heard Bristol mutter under her breath.

"So, Sutton, how was your day?" my dad began, surprisingly turning to me instead of Bristol. In all of our family conversations, we started with Bristol, and then turned to me if there was any time left. Normally there wasn't anything that I had to say, so it was a good enough system.

"This has been my first full week of tennis camp," I said, reaching forward and grabbing the ketchup. I wanted to tell them about the kids who had attacked Natalie with a racket, about the ridiculous things that parents did, but that was going to cause a fight. "It went really well, actually. The kids were more excited than I thought they would be."

My dad nodded, reaching for his water glass. "And you're going to be able to balance working at this tennis camp with everything else you need to get done this summer?"

"We'll discuss that later," my mom said. "Sutton knows that this is a very important summer for her college applications, and this tennis camp development is new."

"Way to talk about her like she's not even here,"

Bristol said, squeezing the ketchup bottle. A giant pool of red oozed onto her plate next to her burger.

"We just want the best for you," my mom said, scooping a piece of lettuce onto her plate. "That's all."

Silence descended on the table as we ate, only broken by the buzz of a lawnmower next door. "Bristol, we got fantastic news from your physical therapist today," my mom said eventually, breaking the silence. "He thinks that with a lot of hard work, you'll be cleared to play next spring!"

Bristol looked up from her hamburger, narrowing her eyes. "That's your fantastic news?"

"Of course it's fantastic news!" my mom said, starting to reach a hand towards Bristol. "I know it's longer than you wanted for your return, but it's great progress."

"I don't care! I'm done playing lacrosse!" She banged her hand against the side of the table. The ketchup spilled over the side of her plate and dripped onto the floor..

My hand froze halfway to my plate. Bristol not playing lacrosse was impossible. There couldn't exist a world where Bristol wasn't playing a sport in some way.

But there was, wasn't there? Right now.

"Bristol, I know it's been rough with your injury,

but that seems like an awfully big statement," my dad said, jumping in for my mom. "You love lacrosse."

"You're not listening." Bristol stood up, shoving her chair back.

"Of course we're listening!" My mom shook her head.

Bristol turned and looked me straight in the eyes. "Sutton, since these people won't listen to me, maybe I'll just tell you."

I froze in place, Bristol's eyes digging into mine. "I didn't go to the hospital because I accidentally took too many pills. I took the pills on purpose, and for the first time, Mia wasn't there to stop me."

That couldn't be true. I would have known. She was my sister. I couldn't have missed that with my own sister.

"But Mia came back just in time," Bristol said, her eyes on me. "She called an ambulance immediately. She knew I was spiraling. She was the one who made sure I got to my therapy appointments. The health center at school literally prescribed antidepressants to me, but I couldn't get them without my parents' insurance. And Mom and Dad just thought that I should sleep more and maybe not take chemistry."

"I'm sorry," I whispered.

Bristol's eyes met mine. "I have felt this way since

high school. I've had anxiety attacks and many, many times where I've felt like I'm sinking into a dark hole. But no one will talk about it. No one ever asked, and no one wanted to admit that I wasn't perfect."

Bristol took a deep breath. I reached my hand out, laying it gently on her arm. I didn't have anything to say. There wasn't anything I could say. I had somehow missed it all.

"I tried to commit suicide. And all you will talk about is lacrosse!" Bristol said finally. She pushed in her chair and turned back into the house.

My mom and dad clattered after her. "Bristol! Come back!" my dad called. She was getting away from my parents yet again, out the door and into her car..

I got out my phone and dialed Mia's number. It rang out to voicemail. "Mia," I said, hearing the beg in my voice. "Bristol just told me. Come back, please. I need you. We need you."

I heard a car engine. I ran to the front door to see Bristol pulling away in her car outside.

I grabbed my keys and jumped into my car, turning it on. I headed straight downtown, driving double the speed limit and blowing through three stop signs on the way. I had to find someone who could help. I'd failed Bristol before, but I wouldn't fail this time.

I ran straight up to the counter at Starbucks, where Mia was standing in her green apron. "Sutton?" she asked, her eyebrows shooting up.

"I need your help. Bristol just fought with my parents, and I don't know what to do," I blurted out all at once.

Mia reached across the counter and put her hand on my shoulder. "Breathe, Sutton," she said softly. "It's going to be okay."

She glanced over at one of her coworkers, who nodded. "Go ahead, Mia, I'll cover for you," her coworkers said, and Mia mouthed something in reply. She took off her apron, then stepped out around the counter.

"Okay. So can you tell me what happened?" Mia said, putting her hand on my shoulder.

"Bristol told me what happened, then yelled at my parents, and then she jumped into her car and drove off," I replied. I wasn't even sure if I was saying whole words, or if everything was just coming out in a rush.

Mia took a deep breath. "Okay. Let's go."

We climbed into the car. Mia took the wheel, tapping me on the knee briefly. "It's okay, Sutton. None of this is your fault."

But it was my fault, wasn't it? Sisters were

supposed to be able to tell these kinds of things. I should have known.

Mia started driving. I didn't question where she was driving. If anyone knew Bristol, it had to be Mia.

"How did you know what had happened?" I asked her. "How were you able to tell when the rest of us couldn't?"

Mia sighed, keeping her foot on the accelerator. "I don't know, Sutton. I just talked to her, and when she answered, I listened."

I closed my eyes as Mia took the next turn too fast, the car tires screeching. We pulled into the parking lot for the town beach.

"Stay in the car," Mia said to me, opening her door and stepping out. She jogged across the beach, and in the distance, I could see the silhouette of another person. Mia stopped, wrapping her arms around the figure. I closed my eyes as they started to walk, slowly, together, back to the car.

SEVEN

I stared at my ceiling.

I didn't want to go to my internship. I couldn't get up and go downstairs like everything was normal. It had been a whole twelve hours since family dinner, and I wasn't ready to get out of bed and face the day.

If my image of Bristol had been cracked before, it was shattered now. I was only sitting there because of Bristol, and now, I didn't know if I wanted that. I had spent my life trying to be Bristol, but Bristol didn't want to be Bristol.

I pulled on a polo shirt and khakis, staring at myself in the mirror again. This wasn't me. Maybe I wasn't pink-hair Natalie, but I wasn't polo shirt girl either.

I closed my eyes and took a deep breath. I pulled my hair back into a simple ponytail, then walked downstairs to see my parents sitting at the kitchen counter.

"Good morning," I said, reaching into the fruit bowl and picking up a banana.

"Good morning, Sutton," my dad said back. His hand was resting on my mom's back. She blinked at me a few times, then looked away.

I had the feeling that I'd stumbled into a scene that I wasn't meant to see. I took a deep breath. "I'm going to work now if you guys need me for anything."

"Thank you for telling us, Sutton," my dad said. I nodded and walked out through the front door.

Last night, Mia had driven back with Bristol in the car. Bristol had immediately gone up to her room when we pulled into the driveway, escorted by Mia. My mom had tried to follow, but Mia had shook her head. "Not right now. She doesn't want to talk to you right now."

"But I'm her mother!" my mom had yelled at Mia. Mia had just followed Bristol into her room, locking the door behind them. My mom had stood outside the room, staring at the shut door.

I wondered for a second if Mia was going to be at Starbucks today, then realized that she'd probably called off. I wanted to track her down and find out what really happened, hear the story from someone else who'd been there and who'd understand.

I drove through town to my internship, fiddling with the radio. How had I missed this? How, in all the years I'd lived with Bristol, had I not noticed anything? Looking back, I couldn't tell if I was making up the signs or seeing them for the first time. One time she'd been so tired that she hadn't made it to lacrosse practice, but was that because she had depression or because she was just actually tired from everything she did?

I pulled into the parking lot. This internship felt pointless on a normal day. I was supposed to sit there and file documents like my entire world hadn't fallen apart.

I grabbed my bag and walked in, through the hallway and into my windowless room. I opened my laptop and just stared at it. I couldn't bring myself to open a document and just start on it.

"Sutton?" Bethany walked up behind me, holding her iced coffee in front of her. "Where are we with our email campaigns? I sent you an email last night and you never responded."

I had forgotten about those. Not that I would have worked on them last night anyway. "I had something personal. I'll do them later."

Bethany's nostrils flared for a second. "What do you mean?"

"I mean that I didn't do them last night because I

had something come up." I'd never spoken to an adult like this before, but it didn't even scare me now.

Bethany pursed her lips, still holding her iced coffee in front of me. Water condensed on the side and dripped down onto my leg. "I'm not sure you understand responsibility, Sutton. You knew that you were supposed to complete those last night, and you're giving me excuses. I've been very flexible with you."

"It's happened one time!" Not that I cared about the stupid emails, but I had done everything else she'd asked this summer. I'd hustled to get everything done. She couldn't tell me that I wasn't responsible now.

"It's been more than once this summer, Sutton. You came in here wearing inappropriate clothing, and now you're telling me that you haven't finished an assignment," Bethany said. "Your work is not meeting my standards."

That was it. I picked my laptop back up, shoving it into my bag. "I quit."

"You what?" Bethany's mouth opened. "You cannot just walk out of here, Sutton."

I slung my bag over my shoulder and marched to the door. "Actually, I can. That's what I'm doing. Don't bother sending me my paycheck."

And with that, I marched down the windowless

hallway, right out the front door and into the summer heat.

I reached my car in the parking lot. I opened the door and threw my laptop down onto the seat next to me. I dropped into my seat and stared out the windshield. I had actually done it. I had actually quit something for the first time in my life.

This was awesome.

I glanced behind me. I couldn't just sit in the parking lot. It'd ruin my dramatic exit. I couldn't exactly go home and explain to my parents that I'd quit, so that left driving. I turned on my car, found the right playlist on my phone, and started to drive.

Twenty minutes later, I found myself in the backroads of town, where the roads didn't have dividing lines and I was left guessing as to what turns I was supposed to make. I hadn't seen another car in ten minutes, and I could feel my shoulders relaxing.

I saw a figure on the road up ahead as I came around a curve. I slammed on the brakes, heart pounding.

The figure looked up at me. It was Michael in short shorts and a t-shirt, bending down to tie his shoe. "Sutton?" he asked, looking up towards me. "What are you doing here?"

"I've had a really bad day," I blurted out. "And I just rage quit my job."

"Is everything okay?" he asked, walking over to the passenger side and learning in through the open window. He reached for the car door handle, pulling it towards himself. "Open up."

Before I could think about it too much, I hit the unlock button. Michael climbed into the car and glanced down at the angry music playing from my phone. He stared at me for a second, waiting for me to say something.

My stomach rumbled. "You know, I think I might need food," I said finally. Everything felt less overwhelming after you ate.

He laughed, turning towards me and giving me a smile. "Well, I know just the place. Take the next left."

Seven minutes later, we drove into a tiny cul-de-sac, then Michael directed me to turn. "Did you just take me to your house?" I asked, glancing over at Stacey's house next door.

"If you wanted to know the closest place that had food, I directed you right to it," Michael replied, stepping out of the car and unlocking the front door. "Come on in."

I followed him through the front door into a mudroom. It was a mess, to put it nicely. There were family photos on every bit of wall, shoes all over the floor, and jackets left in the corner. Michael kicked off his shoes and walked through the front door, signaling me to follow into the kitchen. He pulled open the fridge and started to slide things towards me. "How does half of a leftover pad Thai sound? It was mine from a couple nights ago, but I'm sure it's still good."

"Honestly, at this point, food poisoning is the least of my worries," I replied, not even fully comprehending the weirdness of the situation. I had dramatically quit my job, and now I was eating Michael's leftover dinner in his kitchen.

"So do you want to talk about things, or do you just need food right now?" he asked.

I stuck a giant mouthful of pad Thai into my mouth. "Just let me appreciate how good this is for a second," I replied.

"You do that, and I'm going to go take the fastest shower ever," Michael replied. "Be back in a second."

I nodded, keeping my focus on the food where it belonged. I barely had time to finish the food before Michael came down the stairs and back into the kitchen. "Are you training for the season already?" I asked, scraping the last noodle out of the container.

"That, and I love it," he said. He opened a bottle of sports drink he'd grabbed from the fridge. "I started running after everything with my dad.. It was like that maybe if I started doing the things that he did, I'd start to understand him more."

Michael dropped the bottle on the counter, and I caught myself staring at him for a second. There was something about him. Maybe it was that he seemed to understand himself, that he didn't seem insecure or awkward. He seemed to move through space with purpose and confidence, the total opposite of how I felt most of the time.

"Then," he continued, twisting the top off the bottle, "once I got out of that stage of grief, I started using running as my way of coping. I'd run for miles and miles, and it made me tired enough that I could actually sleep. When I started to become more okay after everything, I kept running because I found that I actually liked it. And now it's just part of who I am."

I nodded, pushing the takeout container away from me. "I can see that."

"Thanks for not being weird about it," Michael said, pulling out a chair from under the counter and sitting down across from me. "It's sometimes hard to explain to people that I'm not doing this because my dad did it, not any more at least. But people feel like they need to tell me that they remember my dad and that it's okay. Which obviously, I know. But at some point, you have to start doing things for yourself and not only be the person who lost someone. But it takes a while."

"How long is it?" I asked.

"It takes a lot longer than you think," Michael replied, opening the fridge and pulling out another container of leftovers. He ate for a second, then looked up at me. "So what do you want to talk about?"

I took a deep breath and looked down at the counter, focusing on a black blotch in the middle of it. "My sister told me last night that she tried to commit suicide in college, and that my parents knew and haven't done anything."

"That's heavy," Michael said, and I could feel his eyes on me.

"I'm just mad at my parents for not telling me, and upset that Bristol is clearly suffering, and confused that I didn't see it, and confused too because I'd always wanted to be Bristol, you know? Bristol was perfect."

"Bristol seemed perfect," Michael corrected me.

"Yeah, that's what I should have said," I corrected myself. That Bristol had never actually existed. "But how did I miss it?"

"Sutton." I looked up to see Michael looking me directly in the eyes. I felt the weight of his hand start to cover mine. "I pretend I'm okay all the time. I still have bad days, you know? I have days where things hit me again. And they aren't frequent, but I've gotten to the point where sometimes I'm pretending. And most people can't tell."

"But your sister should be able to!" I wasn't blaming Bristol for how she felt. I was blaming myself for not seeing it, I wanted to say to him.

Michael shook his head. "Being related doesn't mean that you will always know everything that's going on in Bristol's mind. You can't blame yourself for that."

I took a deep breath and stared at the ceiling. There were pasta sauce stains up there. "I quit my internship today too."

"Congrats," Michael said, not taking his hand off mine. "I mean, I assume that's a congratulations."

"Honestly, I hated it, so I'm happy," I replied, then shook my head again. "Michael. I literally just took my laptop, told her I quit, and walked out the door."

"That's gutsy," Michael said "You should be proud of yourself."

"I don't feel badass right now. I just feel tired," I replied. The adrenaline from the day had started to wear off. I was going to have to face the consequences soon.

"I think that's natural after the kind of week

you've had." Michael shook his head, a couple water droplets from his hair hitting me in the face. "You deserve a week off."

"I wish I could just take a week off from my life." I shook my head. At the moment, what I wanted was nothing more than a Disney movie and a giant bowl of popcorn. I looked up at Michael, a sudden thought hitting me. "Actually, do you happen to have Netflix?"

I HEADED BACK to my house around five. I'd hung out with Michael, watching dumb movies and throwing popcorn at the screen, until he'd had to head out to pick up his sister. I'd forgotten everything that was waiting for me at my house. Things just seemed easier with him.

I drove up, spotting Bristol's car parked in the driveway. Mia must have just gotten home from work. I walked into the house. My mom was standing in the kitchen, her arms crossed, staring at Mia.

"Hi," I said, putting my bag down on the counter. My mom didn't turn around to face me.

"Mia," I heard her say, her voice clipped, "I appreciate how much you care about Bristol, but I think that it's time that you headed back home."

"What do you mean?" Mia asked, taking half a

step back and crossing her arms. She was staring right at my mom, her eyes narrowing.

"I think that Bristol has gone through a very difficult period in her life. While I appreciate that you've been there for her so far, I think that it's time for her to be with her family." My mom wasn't even forcing a smile.

"But she's my best friend." Mia's arms tightened over her chest. "I need to be here for her. She's finally getting better, and she'd be way better if she got on her meds."

"Bristol has lots of friends from high school here who can support her," my mother replied, resting a hand on the counter.

"What's going on?" I asked, standing up straighter. "Mom? Mia?"

"Sutton, this doesn't concern you," my mom said, her voice still clipped. "You can head upstairs."

"No, it does," I said, my voice cracking. "Mom, Mia's great. She's the only person that Bristol talks to." And even if I wanted that person to be me, I wanted to make sure that my sister was better more. I needed Bristol, and Bristol needed Mia. It was that simple.

"Sutton!" my mom snapped, her voice jumping to a shout. "Enough."

I froze in place. My mom had never yelled at me

before. Been disappointed, sure, but never yelled. We didn't yell in this family. We couched everything in artificial politeness.

"Bristol's father and I know what's best for her." Mia looked like she was about to open her mouth. My mom shook her head. "We will fix this situation. It's time that you let us handle it as the adults."

Mia's mouth opened and shut without noise. "Please go upstairs and get your things," my mom continued, holding her arm stiffly in front of her towards the stairs.

"Mom," I managed, staring at her. Mia left the room, her flip flops hitting the floor like little gunshots. "Mom, what are you doing?"

"Sutton, I am not negotiating this." She turned away from me back towards the kitchen counter, as though I wasn't there.

"Are you serious?" I asked, my voice getting higher. "You heard Bristol yesterday!"

"It was an accident, Sutton!" my mom snapped, turning back towards me. "Bristol needs a regular schedule, rest, and her family to support her. She was much happier in high school when we provided all those things. This is clearly her not adjusting well to college."

I heard Mia coming down the stairs. I ran outside. There had to be a way that I could stop this somehow. Mia was the only person who could reach Bristol. Mia walked outside, a suitcase in her hands. "Mia," I breathed.

She shook her head, not looking at me. "Don't, Sutton. There's nothing that you can do."

"But – " I started.

Mia stared out at the road. "You know what? If your parents don't want me here, then they don't want me here. There's nothing I'm going to do that's going to change your mom's mind. She's hated me since she met me."

"But you're better than any of her other friends!" Bristol's other friends hadn't come to visit. They hadn't been here.

"And?" Mia turned towards me. "Stop, Sutton. You can keep saying nice things, but it's not going to change anything."

My dad's car pulled into the driveway. The passenger side door opened, and Bristol stepped out.

"Mia?" Bristol demanded, seeing Mia standing in the driveway with her beaten up suitcase, my mother standing in the doorway behind her, her arms crossed. There was silence as Bristol glanced from my mom to Mia and back again. "Mom?" Bristol said, taking a step towards her. "What's going on here? Why is Mia standing in the driveway?"

"Bristol," my mom said, her voice breaking. "Bristol, I need you to – "

"No, I don't need to do anything! Why is Mia standing outside in the driveway with her suitcase?" Bristol glanced back at Mia. They exchanged a quick look, and it was clear that Bristol knew exactly what was happening.

"What the hell are you doing?" Bristol said, whipping over to face my mom. "I invited Mia. She's here because she cares about me!"

"Bristol, we're your family," my mom said, her voice finally slipping a little bit.

Bristol spun away from my mom, and I was sure she was going to scream. Mia put her hand on Bristol's arm. There was something invisible that passed in between them, and Bristol nodded her head slightly.

A taxi pulled up in front of the house. "Mia, your car is here," my mom said, pointing towards the car, her eyes hard.

Mia pulled her lips together, picking up her bag and walking to the end of the driveway. Bristol ran after her, faster than I thought Bristol would ever be able to run again. As Mia stepped into the car, Bristol watching her go, then seemed to crumple at the end of the driveway, her shoulders slouching and her entire body seeming to lose air.

We all stood there for a second, my mom in the doorway of the house, my dad standing at his car, me frozen in the middle.

"Why don't we all go get some dinner?" my mom said, shutting the house door behind her. "It'll be nice if we get out of the house a little bit, don't you think?"

My dad made uneasy eye contact with my mom and then nodded. "Bristol, I'm sure that you're hungry from physical therapy today. Let's go get some burgers as a family."

Bristol gave me a look that clearly meant that she could think of nothing worse than having to get burgers with the rest of the family. But with our car keys locked in the house, there was no option but to get in the car. I glanced back at the house, realizing my phone was lying on the kitchen counter, but then gave up and walked to the car.

Bristol slammed the door next to me, and I glanced over at her. I wanted to say something, anything, but the words failed me again. Dad turned on the car and started the drive, turning on the radio to cover the silence.

Dad parked the car in front of the burger restaurant that we'd always gone to when we were growing up. There were outdoor tables with bright red and white striped umbrellas over them, and my mom immediately smiled. "Look, girls. We can get one of the tables outside like we always used to."

I glanced over at Bristol, who still hadn't said anything. I wanted to ask her what was running through her mind but just stayed quiet.

My dad walked out and talked to the host at the stand, and we were immediately seated at one of the outside tables. The waiter dropped off the menus, smiling at us. "Great night for sitting outside, isn't it?"

My mom smiled, relieved to make small talk. Another family walked by, old friends of my parents from when they spent every weekend in the stands at yet another lacrosse game. "It's so nice to see the whole Greer family out enjoying the sunshine," the mom said to my mom.

"Yes, we're just enjoying the nice weather with our daughters," my mom said, smiling up at them. "So good to see you here. Have a nice dinner."

We sat in silence until the waiter came back to take our orders. "I'll have salad with salmon," my mom said, passing back the menu.

Bristol looked up at the waiter. "Bristol Greer?" he asked. "I didn't know you were home for the summer."

She shrugged. "Yeah. I unfortunately don't really have another option, so I'm here."

My mom's face tightened, but the waiter nodded. "I know what you mean. It's weird to come home after college and start living with your parents again, you know?"

My parents glanced at each other, and I was pretty sure I could see the silent conversation passing between them. "What do you want?" the waiter asked, shifting his weight slightly. I recognized it as the stance that guys always took talking to Bristol, slightly intimidated, slightly unsure of themselves.

"The salad is very good," my mom said, leaning forward towards Bristol. "They make all the dressings by hand here."

"Yeah, I'll have a salad," Bristol said, and what looked like relief flitted across my mom's face. Bristol glanced up at the waiter. "Kidding, obviously. Can I get a double patty burger with bacon, barbecue sauce, Swiss cheese, avocado, and mushrooms?"

"And do you want fries with that?" the waiter asked, noting it on his pad and seeming even more impressed with Bristol than he had been a minute ago.

"Yeah. I want a double order of nacho fries. Extra cheese sauce and bacon bits," she said, passing him back her menu

"Um, I'll just have the burger with blue cheese," I

said as the waiter turned towards me, still clearly impressed by Bristol's order.

"Don't even think you're going to get to steal my nacho fries," Bristol replied. "Get your own."

Somehow, this felt like a conversation about more than nacho fries. "Can I get the fully loaded sweet potato fries, actually?" I glanced back at Bristol. "No stealing."

Bristol nodded, and it felt like a pact of some sort. We sat in silence for another minute, Bristol slurping down her iced tea just loudly enough that I knew she was doing it to be annoying. As soon as we were mad at our parents, we turned back into the people we were in middle school. We slurped our drinks, knowing that that was the only weapon we had left.

"Hi, Sutton," Stacey said behind me. I turned around to see her walking by my table with her family in tow. Everyone was out tonight.

"Hi there!" I said. Stacey's eyes went from me to Bristol and back, clearly sensing the weirdness. I cleared my throat. "There are so many people here."

"I know. Apparently I wasn't the only one craving loaded fries tonight," she said, looking directly at me like she wanted to let me know she understood.

I glanced at Bristol, who didn't say anything. "Anyway," Stacey said, tapping me on the shoulder,

"I'll let you get back to dinner. Text me later?" She glanced from me back towards my parents, her eyes softening.

"Yeah, sounds good." I'd have to tell her the details later. There was nothing about this situation that felt like a normal family dinner.

"Is that Stacey Chapman?" my mom asked, leaning towards me. "She was always a very nice girl."

"Yeah. She's – " Oh, screw it. "She works at tennis camp with me."

"Oh." My mom nodded, and it was like I could see the fight in her mind. Tennis camp was bad, but Stacey Chapman being back in my life had to be good. "I'm glad that you're spending time with your friends this summer in between all of your other activities. You know how important it is to build a social life full of people who support you."

I didn't know how to answer, so I took the same easy way out that I always did and said nothing. Then I slurped my iced tea extra loudly.

"I know that this has been a really tough time for all of us," my dad said, looking over at my mom. "And your mom and I have realized that we need to be more hands on with you. Sutton, you've been hanging out with new friends and not practicing for soccer, and Bristol, your recovery has been off track. We're going to be bringing more structure home."

"I don't want more structure," Bristol said, slurping her iced tea.

"But you were thriving in high school," my dad said, leaning forward again.

"I wasn't happy in high school!" Bristol pushed her seat back.

"Are you sure you're not just remembering incorrectly because you're stressed out?" my mom asked. "You had great friends in high school. Remember how happy you'd be when you won a lacrosse game?"

Bristol cut my mom off before she could say anything else. "I remember being in my dorm room and thinking that it would never get better. That even if my therapist finally told me what I had and that we could fix it, I didn't think we could." Bristol's voice was now loud enough that people at the tables around us were turning and looking, trying and failing to hide their curiosity.

My mom's face was devoid of color. "And you know what?" Bristol said, standing up and shoving her seat in. "I was happy when I tore my ACL. I was actually happy. Because it meant that I finally got to leave lacrosse behind. I could finally stop being Bristol the lacrosse star and do what I actually wanted to do."

"Bristol, please," my dad choked out.

"If you're not going to listen, then I'm not going to stay here. You've already kicked out the one person who did listen." Bristol's voice had started to shake. She pushed her chair in, walking out of the front of the restaurant. My parents stared at each other, mouths open, my mom at a loss for words for the first time in her life.

I glanced into the doorway of the restaurant. Stacey was standing there, her mouth open.

I looked back at my parents, and then at Stacey, and then I did the only thing that made any sense to me at the moment. I ran.

I RAN, as fast as I could, back to Bristol. It didn't take long to catch her. "Bristol?" I asked, running up alongside her. She still couldn't run, not on her leg, and we sat down on the sidewalk outside the restaurant.

"Let's get out of here," she said, her voice low. "I don't have my phone. Can you call a cab?"

Shit. "I don't either." It was in my tote bag on the counter at home. I should have gone in and gotten it before we had to run. I couldn't go back in there and ask our parents.

But then, I heard Stacey's voice behind me. "Sutton? Bristol?"

"Stacey!" A wave of relief hit me. Stacey ran towards us, leaning forward and wrapping me in a hug. I closed my eyes for a second. Then I swallowed. "I'm sorry, but can you take us home?"

Stacey took a step back, looking from me to Bristol and then back again. She looked me directly in the eyes and nodded. "Of course. That's what friends are for."

It was the quietest car ride I'd ever been in. Stacey dropped us right in front of the house, sending me a look that meant she was ready when I was ready to talk. I didn't know how to say thank you, so I just gave her the tightest hug I could.

When we finally got home, I grabbed my phone from downstairs. The front was all messages. A few from Bristol's old friends, asking me if Bristol had changed her number, but more importantly, texts from Stacey and Natlaie and Nora and Michael.

I stared at all of them but felt too tired to answer. But the texts kept coming, through the night and into the next day –

Michael – *I heard from Stacey that things with your family got rough today. Want to FaceTime?*

The group chat with Natalie and Nora. Natalie

– *Sutton! Are you there? Is everything okay? Stacey said something happened?*

Then Nora – *And obviously if you don't want to talk about things, it's fine, but we can also talk about things. Don't be scared off by overenthusiastic Natalie please*

Then Natalie again – *we just want you to know that we're thinking about you and love you and sending all the good vibes. Also please tell me what happened so I'll stop worrying!! Stacey was super vague and now I'm all concerned*

Nora again – *NATALIE. Not appropriate*

Natalie – *Sorry!! We love you!*

But the texts that had come in late that night were the ones that meant the most somehow.

Michael – *if you don't want to talk, I totally understand. Sometimes talking is tough. But I'm here for you even if that means we have to watch my sister's copy of Frozen again*

Michael – *seriously, whatever it is, you can tell me and let it gooooooooo*

Coonor – *okay, sorry, that was a bad joke. But I'm always here for you*

Michael – *it's not okay right now. It'll be okay soon.*

I stared at the last text he'd sent. I was lying in bed, the moonlight starting to filter into my room, trying to sleep and staring at my phone instead. It's not okay right now. It'll be okay soon.

I screenshotted the text and set it as my phone background, chanting it to myself under my breath. There was nothing else that could have come close to saying the right thing. I just wanted to be seen. I wanted someone to tell me that it was okay to be sad and mad and everything else at the same time.

I closed my eyes, trying to will myself to sleep again. *It's not okay right now. It'll be okay soon,* I whispered to myself until I finally fell asleep.

EIGHT

I had never been in a house so quiet before.

My parents had vanished into their rooms. If I walked down the hallway, I could hear my mom on the phone at all hours of the day. When I walked past Bristol's room, I'd hear angry music and FaceTime.

I pulled on a pair of gym shorts and tied my hair back into a ponytail, rubbing sunscreen on my face. Without even the excuse of my internship, there were just too many hours that I could spend at the house.

I was about to walk downstairs and grab my tennis stuff when I paused at the top of the stairs. I looked back at the hallway, the beige carpeting and the white walls, the silence only broken by the occasional murmur from one of the rooms. I turned around and walked over to Bristol's door, knocking once.

I heard clattering inside, then nothing. "Bristol?" I asked through the door, softly enough that my parents couldn't overhear.

The door opened slightly. I peered around the corner to see Bristol beckoning me in. I walked into her room, which was definitely in better shape than at the start of the summer. There was a pile of pizza boxes in the corner, but over it, Bristol had opened a window.

She'd redecorated, too. The lacrosse medals were all gone, replaced by printouts of photos. As I glanced closer, I could see that all of them were from college – Bristol with Mia, Bristol with a group of guys in tight neon pants, Bristol making faces at the camera laughing.

"What's up?" Bristol asked, perching on the edge of her bed.

"Do you want to come to tennis camp with me?" I blurted out, pulling my attention away from the photos.

Bristol let out a short laugh, gathering her hair and sticking it up into a ponytail. "I tore my ACL a few months ago, remember that?"

"You don't have to play or do anything but sit in the clubhouse and drink their weird off-brand sodas,"

I replied. "I just thought, maybe you wanted to get out of the house for a little bit."

Bristol looked around her room. "Screw it. Can't be more boring than sitting here."

It took a little bit of sneaking around, but we managed to get out of the house without my parents noticing. Twenty minutes later, as we pulled up to the tennis club, I glanced over at Bristol. "I guess before we go in, I should tell you that I teach tennis here now." I shrugged "Okay, that's kind of an exaggeration. I don't really teach tennis so much as I run around the court trying to keep kids from hitting each other with rackets. It's not nearly as glamorous as it sounds."

"Don't worry, it didn't sound glamorous," Bristol replied, and I thought I could start to see a hint of a smile on her face.

"Well, if it seems like people here know me, that's why," I said, tucking the car keys into my pocket and getting out. "You've been warned."

Bristol stepped out of the car as well, shaking out her ponytail. "Honestly, I wouldn't mind hearing a few Sutton horror stories. I don't think I've ever heard one of those since you pooped your pants in preschool."

"You heard Mom and Dad talking about my

internship." My one moment of rebellion was getting me so much crap.

She shook her head and unbuckled her seatbelt. "God, I wish I could have done that. I got so sick of Bethany asking me to scan files. I literally scanned the same thing five weeks in a row, and she never noticed."

It appeared that the real Bristol had not been the ideal intern, which made me happier than it should have. We walked into the clubhouse, almost running into somebody else running down the hallway. The figure drew to a fast stop, and I looked up to see Michael. Of course. "Oh, sorry, Sutton!" he said, his face flushing slightly. "I wasn't really looking where I was going. I'm Michael, by the way," he said, sticking his hand out for Bristol to shake.

She reached out and shook it. "I'm Bristol. Sutton's sister."

"Oh yeah, you knew my dad," Michael said, brushing his hair out of his face. I should have remembered. Michael's dad had been the guy who brought Bristol into lacrosse, the only coach she'd ever truly clicked with. Bristol had sobbed at his funeral and written her college essay about him.

"I did," Bristol said eventually, nodding slightly. "He was a real one."

"He was," Michael said. I glanced over at him,

waiting for the grief to show on his face, but nothing did. "So what are you guys doing here?"

"Sutton thinks we're here to play tennis, but secretly, we're just here to get that really delicious off-brand grape Fanta that they stock in all the vending machines," Bristol replied. "What can I say? I've been thinking about it ever since I went off to college."

Michael started to laugh, then glanced over at me, almost like he wanted to be sure that I was laughing too. "I mean, I should let you guys have your grape Fantas," he said, glancing at me before turning back towards Bristol.

Bristol shook her head. "No, you guys go play." Michael started to say something, so Bristol shook her head more vigorously. "Seriously. I had ACL surgery a few months ago. There's no tennis in my life right now, but there will be off-brand grape Fanta soon."

"If you're sure," I said again. Bristol raised an eyebrow at me, then headed off towards the hallway with the legendary grape soda.

"So," Michael said as we walked out to the court, bouncing a tennis ball up and down off the ground. "I wasn't expecting to see you and Bristol out here."

"My house is awful right now. Nobody talks to one another. And my parents kicked Mia out."

"I heard from Stacey that things were rough,"

Michael replied, tossing me the tennis ball. I caught it with one hand and started to bounce it off the ground. "I texted you, but I didn't hear back, so I figured you were going through some stuff."

"I'm sorry," I said, the words feeling inadequate. Michael had cared enough about me to text me, and apparently I couldn't even manage a 'Sorry, can't talk right now' in reply.

"You don't have to apologize for not answering my text," Michael replied, tossing the tennis ball up and down. "I just wanted to make sure you were okay."

"I'm okay. We're okay," I replied, the ball continuing to bounce off the ground. I started hitting it harder, glad for the excuse to not have to look at Michael directly.

"You can always talk to me, if you want," Michael said, his face flushing.

"Thanks," I said, making eye contact for a second too long.

I couldn't be flirting with Michael. Michael was the guy I'd told entirely too many embarrassing things to for him to be attracted to me. The only type of guys who ever liked me were guys like Dylan – people looking for someone where they knew exactly what they were going to get. People who were looking for significant others who stood behind them and cheered them on, who understood that it was just high school and we had lots of other priorities, people who weren't looking to have their lives radically changed.

Dylan. Right. Michael couldn't be flirting with me, because I had a boyfriend out there.

At the moment, it didn't feel like Dylan and I were together. I hadn't told him about all of the Bristol stuff, and I hadn't heard from him for two weeks. I wasn't sure how to start the conversation about everything that had happened, so I just hadn't texted him.

You deserve more than this. I wasn't sure whose voice it was in the back of my head, Michael or Mia or Stacey or Natalie or Nora. Maybe it was finally mine, but it was shouting it at me. I deserved more than this from a boyfriend. Checking the box wasn't enough for me any more.

I swallowed and looked back towards Michael, trying to shove those thoughts away for later. One more thing to figure out.

"Bristol seems like she's doing okay," Michael said, bringing my focus back to our conversation. "And I know that you can't tell what's really going on with people from talking to them for five minutes, but she seems really cool."

"She is pretty cool. Growing up, she was basically everything I aspired to be," I said.

"And she isn't any more?" he asked.

I shook my head, still bouncing the tennis ball. "It's hard to say. I guess I always thought of her as the person who had everything figured out, and now that everything's happened, it's clear that I was wrong. I was just looking at the outside with everyone else."

"But she's still your sister," Michael said.

"Do you know who I'm actually pissed at?" I asked, gesturing to him on the other side of the court. I reached up and slammed the ball as hard as I could towards the other side, taking a deep grunt as I did so. That felt good. "My parents. Bristol wants to go to therapy. She wants to be on medication. She knows what she wants and she's saying it!"

Michael chased after the ball and gently thrown it back to me over the net. I slammed it as hard as I could again, watching it sail past the end of the court and clang loudly into a fence.

Another ball, another full body smack. "It's like my parents just think she can fix it with getting her routine back. It's like they don't understand that Bristol's mind is just backfiring on her." Michael threw me another ball, and I smacked it again. I caught my breath as I brought my arm back. It just felt good to move, to physically get the anger out. "It's like she tore her ACL, and nobody is talking about how if my parents had sent her to a better college, this wouldn't have happened. Everyone understands that sometimes you break your leg and you need surgery and medicine. But not when it comes to mental things, for some reason."

Another hit. I felt it through my whole body this time. Terrible form, but it felt good to move. "Sorry," I said, exhaling sharply and bending over. "I'm so frustrated with my family. If Mia is the person who's making Bristol feel better, then they shouldn't kick Mia out. And if Bristol doesn't want to play lacrosse any more, she shouldn't have to."

"Maybe that's part of college, you know. You get away and figure all that out," Michael said.

Maybe that had been part of it for Bristol. Everyone in town knew Bristol for who she'd always been. There wasn't a way for Bristol to figure out who she really was when everyone thought they knew the answer. She was Bristol Greer, class president and captain of the lacrosse team.

But in college, she could have been anyone. For everything Mia knew, the day Bristol showed up to college and moved into their room, she could have been the least athletic, least popular person in her high school.

Maybe Bristol and I weren't all that different. Maybe we were both unhappy with who we were and looking to change. But I hadn't left for college yet.

"Sutton?" I turned around to see Stacey jogging over towards us. "Oh hey, Michael."

"Hi, Stacey," Michael said, bouncing the tennis ball he'd run over to retrieve up and down. "I didn't know you were coming over, or I would have offered you a ride."

"No worries," Stacey shook her head. She looked at me, raising an eyebrow. "Sutton?"

I owed her more than a brush off answer. "I'm okay. Things with my family are kind of rough, but I think we're going to get through it." Michael was still looking at me, and I could feel his eyes on the side of my face. Somehow that felt more personal than before.

"Of course you'll get through it," Stacey said. "Do you want to talk?"

I shook my head. "I think I'm still figuring out what I want to say, honestly. Things were intense."

"You know that's what friends are for, right?" Stacey asked. "Ice cream, fashion advice, and talking through things."

"You've never given me fashion advice," Michael said, raising an eyebrow at Stacey.

"You'd ignore my fashion advice if I gave it," Stacey replied. "Michael, I've never seen you in anything but shorts and a running top. You used to wear shorts in the middle of the winter, remember?"

"Shut up, Stacey," Michael replied, but he was grinning.

"You know, I'm here for you if you want to talk," Stacey said, nudging my side gently. "I have to go do some camp stuff now, but you two have fun."

"We will!" I called back. I looked up at Michael, feeling my stomach squeeze together as though I'd been on a roller coaster. "Should we actually go play tennis now?"

An hour later, we were both drenched in sweat. "That was great," Michael said, giving me a fist bump as I bent over to catch my breath. "You're actually really good at this."

"Is that a backhanded compliment?" I asked, twisting my head to look up at him and feeling my stomach lurch slightly as we made eye contact.

"If it was a backhanded compliment, it was a compliment as strong as your backhand in that last game there. How's that for a pivot?" he said, tossing the last ball we'd hit up and down in the air.

"Not as good as your back foot pivot in that last game," I shot back, then grinned.

"See you around later?" he asked, starting to reach towards my arm and then pulling his hand back.

"Sounds good," I replied, then headed into the clubhouse to see how Bristol was doing. To my surprise, she was talking to Stacey, her leg propped up on a chair, one of the terrible off-brand grape Fantas next to her.

"Hey, Sutton," Bristol said, looking up at me as I walked in. "You look gross."

"Thanks. It's hot out," I replied, glancing around for a towel. No luck.

"Do you and Michael normally play together?" Stacey asked.

I shook my head quickly. "No, just sometimes when I run into him. I just came to hang out with Bristol this morning."

"Correction. I just came for this amazing off-brand Fanta, which Stacey was nice enough to get for me after I realized that I didn't have any quarters," Bristol said, raising her can of grape soda.

Stacey smiled at me. "I have the keys to all of the vending machines. I don't think I've ever seen anyone actually take anything from the machines before, though, so you do so at your own risk."

Bristol laughed. "You can tell I haven't been here in a while, because otherwise, I would have gotten every single one of them just for the joy of making Sutton drink them. It's basically our early childhood in a can."

"Well, you can have the rest of them in the vending machine then. Otherwise, I think I might have to throw them away as a public service." I could hear a phone ring in one of the further away rooms, and Stacey glanced over her shoulder. "Gotta go answer that. I'll see you around!"

"Bye!" I called to Stacey as she bounded away, her ponytail bouncing up and down.

"So I assume that you want to go home and shower?" Bristol asked, glancing up and down at me. There was a small pool of sweat forming under where I was standing, and I shivered in the air conditioning.

"Do you want to get ice cream first?" I asked. Maybe it was being out and about, but after being in the fresh air and out of the deathly silence of our house, I wasn't ready to go back.

"I should totally have ice cream now. And I haven't been to Brittany's this summer," Bristol replied, standing up and stretching. "Did I tell you that Mia refused to take me after I told her about the flavors?"

"I can't imagine why. Let's go."

"YOU KNOW, I LIKE YOUR FRIENDS," Bristol said after we reached the ice cream place. We were sitting on a bench overlooking the water. "I didn't realize you had many friends, to be honest."

"I've been trying to make them this summer," I said, taking a bite of ranch dressing and carrot ice cream. It was not quite as horrible as it could have been, but that was a low bar. I didn't understand the people who put ranch on everything. Ranch wasn't even good on carrots, let alone on ice cream.

My other scoop was sriracha and roasted corn flavored, so I wasn't exactly looking forward to that one, either. I snapped a picture and sent it to Natalie and Nora, then realized that I owed them more than a picture of ice cream.

Hey guys, I typed into the group chat, *sorry. I should have gotten back to you guys sooner. Thanks for asking. Things are rough but they'll be okay soon. And I love you too*

My phone dinged immediately with a text from Natalie. *Love you as much as Nora hates mint. And is that lobster bisque??*

"Good friends," Bristol said, glancing over at me as I checked my phone.

"I guess," I replied, trying the sriracha one. It actually wasn't too bad. "I don't know. It feels like some people make friends easily, and I don't have a friend like Mia."

"If you're lucky enough to have a friend like Mia,

you grab onto her with both arms and you never let her go," Bristol replied. "Or them go. I can't presume the gender identity of your best friend."

"How did you know Mia was your best friend?" I asked. The two of them were so different that it was hard for me to picture it sometimes.

Bristol laughed and looked away for a second. "On the first day on campus, there was this huge student activity fair. Mia signed me up for every single thing there. I'd told her that I wasn't sure what I wanted to get involved with on campus, so she decided that it was her mission to help me figure it out. The running coach was after me for weeks."

I could imagine the legions of groups all chasing Bristol, all trying to convince her to join their team. It sounded like high school.

"And eventually, I told Mia that I'd had a rough time with depression and anxiety in high school. I'd always been so high-functioning that I didn't know what to do when I was no longer defined by my sport, and it freaked me out." Bristol shook her head. "And you know what Mia did? She walked with me to the health center and sat in the waiting room while I talked to a therapist for the first time. I thought it was normal to feel like I couldn't breathe sometimes. And Mia told me it was okay to not be okay for the first time ever. She taught me to put myself first."

"Put yourself first?" I asked, a drip of ice cream melting and running over my hand.

Bristol nodded. "I had to learn to take care of myself before I could worry about other things. Because you know what it's like in high school. Everyone tells you to worry about college and grades and extracurriculars and then on top of that your friends and dating and everything else. It's exhausting. And every time I started to go down that path, Mia would remind me that my job was to take care of Bristol. Not my grades, not sports, but Bristol."

"And that's how you knew?"

Bristol laughed. "That's a long story, all of it. It sounds kind of ridiculous even to me when I say it, but Sutton, if you find someone who will be your friend through thick and thin, the kind of friend who's going to make sure you're okay, even if they have to drive six hours in traffic to do it, then you never let that person go."

I thought about Stacey and Michael, about the texts lighting up my phone, about the times this summer where for the first time I'd finally felt like someone out there saw Sutton Greer, not just Bristol Greer's younger sister. I nodded. "I think I know what you mean."

NINE

My phone vibrated, and I rolled over in bed to check who it was. Dylan. *I'm in town today, do you want to get lunch before I go back to camp?*

Disappointment hit me, like I was sad that it was Dylan and not one of my friends.

I hadn't talked to Dylan in what felt like months. We'd traded a few texts, but they'd all been pretty standard – me asking how his day was going, and him telling me about the latest thing that he'd done at lacrosse camp. The deepest our conversation had gotten was when he asked me if I'd been studying for the SATs.

The SATs were about the furthest thing from my mind right now, but I'd told him that I was studying anyway. I had agonized for a while about what to write, but then settled on *things that have been pretty busy here.*

Dylan had immediately written back, *no way as busy as here. Last night, a frog jumped into my window* and proceeded to tell me a long text story about how he'd rescued a frog from his lacrosse gear. I'd thought for a second about calling him or texting him, figuring out some way to get across the point that no, my summer was definitely more dramatic than his, then just shut my phone. Dylan wasn't that kind of boyfriend.

There were reasons I had liked him, I reminded myself as I stood up and stared at my closet. When we'd started dating, there had been plenty of reasons for me to do it. Those reasons just didn't seem all that relevant now.

I still needed to make the effort to get out of bed and look nice, though. I rolled my shoulder and stood up, staring at my closet. Everything felt slightly wrong.

Whatever. There shouldn't be a reason to get dressed up for him. If I needed to pretend for him, then he was the wrong person. I pulled on a t-shirt and jeans, grabbed my car keys, and headed downstairs.

"Sutton?" my mom looked up as I entered the kitchen. It was one of the few times that I saw her anywhere but her room, where she and my dad had sequestered themselves. I heard the coffee machine behind her sputter. She opened her mouth as though she was about to say something, then shook her head. "Where are you heading off to?"

"I'm getting lunch with Dylan," I replied.

"Oh, that's lovely," my mom said, reaching down and putting silverware back into the drawer. "I'm sure you'll get to catch up and hear all about how he's been doing with camp and everything this summer."

Yes, I was sure that I was going to get to hear all about lacrosse camp. I'd be lucky to get a word in edgewise, honestly. I nodded, looking for my car keys and deciding to not say anything.

"Dylan really is such a nice young man," my mom said finally, reaching under the coffee maker to pull her cup out. "I'm glad that you have someone in your life like that. Someone supportive who you can rely on to talk through things."

I was lucky. That was true. I had Stacey and Natalie and Nora and everyone else. I had the people who would pick me up and get ice cream with me.

Maybe I wasn't giving Dylan enough credit. Maybe if I told him about everything that had happened, he'd come back with words of wisdom and a plan. Maybe he'd be able to listen better than Michael and Stacey, able to tell me what I needed to do to get through this. After all, Dylan always seemed to have a plan.

"He is very nice," I replied, tucking my car keys into my pocket and pushing open the front door. "See you later, Mom."

After I left the house, I realized I had time to kill. I parked the car downtown and walked into one of the many boutiques on the main strip. I started to browse through a rack of swimsuits. I heard a clatter in front of me and glanced over the rack to see two older girls standing there, staring down at swimsuits. "Did you hear that Bristol Greer is saying she's never going to play lacrosse again?" one of the girls asked the other.

My stomach clenched, and I took a closer look at the two of them. They looked like they might have been on Bristol's team in high school. There had always been so many people in Bristol's social circle that I could never quite keep up.

"I heard she completely shattered her leg and needs a complete leg reconstruction," the other said back. "That must suck so much. Imagine going D1 and then discovering that you can never play your sport again."

"No, apparently it's even worse." The first girl shook her head. "She lost it last week and screamed at her parents that she'd rather die than ever have to play again."

"No way that's true, and anyway, way to be a drama queen," the second said, lifting her eyes slightly at the first.

"I know, right? Like, it would suck to not be able to play, but I'm not going to run around claiming that I have depression and anxiety because of it. Way to be insensitive to all the people who are actually struggling with mental illness."

What would Natalie do? I could feel the pressure building behind my eyes, the want to scream again.

The two of them laughed and started to walk away. "Hey," I said, the word scratching out of my throat before I could stop it.

"What?" The two of them turned around, looking at me over a rack of overpriced dresses.

I didn't know what I was going to say, what I had planned to say. "Were you talking to us?" the second asked, crinkling her eyebrows.

"Yeah," I managed, the words feeling scratchy, like I hadn't spoken in too long. "It's a pretty asshole move to make fun of someone with mental illness. You never know what people are struggling with under the surface. And just because someone looks like they're doing well doesn't mean that they're okay."

There was a long silence, and I gulped again. "Um, thanks for the tone policing," the first one said, raising her eyebrows at the other and turning away. "Weirdo."

I wanted to tell them that they were the kind of people who were the most damaging. When they said those things so casually, they made it so that Bristol could never talk to them, never have the support that she needed to get through.

I checked the time on my phone. I could probably be early to lunch with Dylan. He'd be squeezing in lunch in between several errands he had to run, so he wouldn't mind if I was early. This almost felt like a formality in some ways, another thing for him to check off his list. Had lunch with Sutton.

I walked into the lunch spot where I was meeting Dylan, finding a table by the window and sitting down. The air conditioning was almost too intense for me after being outside. I had an unpleasant flashback to the office at Bethany's, always being just slightly too cold and just slightly too warm at the same time.

"Sutton!" Dylan walked towards me, dressed in jeans, a t-shirt, and boat shoes. He was handsome in a generic way – wavy brown hair, strong chin, clearly in shape. Nothing exactly stood out about him, but there was that you could point to as an obvious flaw, either.

"Hi, Dylan," I said, getting up and walking around the table to give him a hug. It felt like I was at a college networking event, no butterflies showing up in my stomach. "It's been a while."

"I know, but it's been a really great summer, hasn't it?" Dylan said, pulling out the chair across from mine and flopping into it.

Surprisingly, despite everything, it had been. "What are you doing back here?" I asked, glancing down at the menu in front of me.

"I was supposed to have a week off in between sessions, but then I had the opportunity to extend, so I'm just in town for a couple days," Dylan replied, not looking up from his menu. "Have to pick up stuff before I go back."

"Yeah, that makes sense," I replied, putting my menu to the side and looking at Dylan. "Lacrosse camp sounds like it's been great, though."

That finally made Dylan push his menu to the side and sit up, looking me in the face. "Oh yeah, Sutton. You wouldn't believe how much better I've gotten."

"That's great," I said. One of the wait staff came over, and I ordered the avocado toast and iced latte that I always did. I'd seen Bristol order it when we were out as a family here. As soon as I'd been here without her, I'd stolen the order and made it my own. Iced lattes just felt so adult and sophisticated.

"It's been tough but worth it. No pain, no gain, right?" Dylan continued, drinking half of his water glass in one slug.

"I mean, don't you think there's some benefit to taking it easy?" I asked, twisting my napkin in my lap.

Dylan's eyebrows raised. "Not now. This is one of the most important summers of our lives. What we do this summer can determine where we get into college, and that determines basically the rest of our lives."

"I just think that's a little ridiculous. In the scheme of things, does it really matter if you get into your top choice or not?" Bristol got into all of her top choices. She'd won everything.

Dylan stared at me as though I'd suddenly sprouted a second head. "Of course it matters. If you don't get into a good college, you're not going anywhere in life."

I looked down at my water glass, drawing a pattern in the condensation on the table. "I guess I'm just thinking that maybe that's not the most important thing right now."

Dylan just stared at me still, then shook his head.

"You must really love that tennis camp to be giving up on college completely."

"That's not it. I'm not saying that I'm going to not go to college and become a tennis coach full time. I just like getting to be outside and run around," I replied. "I'm probably not even the best coach. I couldn't be the person who told kids they weren't talented enough, even though they're trying super hard."

"Well, if you don't tell them that, you're basically being cruel," Dylan replied. "If no one tells you the truth, then how are you supposed to pick the sport that you are good at? Imagine playing tennis for fifteen years, and then you go to apply to college, and every single recruiter is like 'nope, not this one, no way does this person have the talent for it.' They're screwed for life."

"Dylan, they're eight years old." I shook my head. "I'm not training the next Roger Federer."

Dylan raised an eyebrow. "Did something happen this summer? Pretty soon, you're going to tell me that you're giving all your tennis kids participation trophies."

I had actually been planning on giving them all participation trophies, because they were eight years old and liked shiny things. Dylan shook his head again. "At least it'll look like good community service on your college applications if you don't tell them you're getting paid."

I closed my eyes briefly, then opened them as the waiter put my iced latte down in front of me. "Thanks," I said, unwrapping my straw and taking the first sip. It felt more and more like Dylan and I were speaking different languages. I couldn't even make him see why I loved tennis camp.

"So how has the rest of your summer been?" Dylan asked, almost like someone was forcing him to ask the considerate question. "Keeping busy training for soccer now that you have all this free time without your internship?"

Ugh. Soccer. I had no desire to play again, but with everything else going on in my life, that concern had taken a back seat. I didn't have time to think through how I could quit soccer without completely devastating my parents.

"I've had a lot of other stuff going on. Personal stuff, and family stuff," I said, pushing the ice cubes in my drink down with my straw. "I've been more focused on that than on a lot of the other college stuff."

"Like what?" Dylan asked.

I took a deep breath and looked up at the ceiling quickly, then back down at Dylan. I had to give him the chance to tell me that he understood. "You know how Bristol is home for the summer?"

"With her ACL. God, that must be the actual worst thing in the world. I can't imagine what it would be like if I injured myself so badly that I couldn't play for an entire season. And she was already going to be their leading scorer." Dylan speared his fork into his food. "So you've been practicing with her to help her get back up to speed?"

Had we ever had a conversation that didn't circle back to lacrosse or college within fifteen seconds? "No, it's been more difficult than that."

"Is she never going to be able to walk again?" Dylan interrupted me. "She's walking again already, though. But did they ban her from playing? I bet she can ignore the doctors if they tell her that. You can't keep her off the field. It's a disservice to the sport."

I opened and closed my mouth. Of course Dylan jumped to what was best for lacrosse as a sport, not what was best for Bristol. "I don't think Bristol wants to play again," I replied finally.

"Come on, Sutton," he said. "Bristol is a champion. She's a literal champion. Everyone knows that. She's obviously going to be upset if she can't play any more."

I didn't know how to tell him how wrong he was. Now that I had actually started to talk to her, I realized how wrong that was. But that was her story to tell, not mine. "I don't think there's any lacrosse in her future," I said finally.

Dylan just looked at me. It was like I could watch the gears in his brain turning over and over and just not clicking. It was like he couldn't actually figure out how someone could opt out of the sport that he loved so much, how anyone could walk away from their high school identity and be happier for it.

"So what does that have to do with you then, if you're not helping her get back on the field?" Dylan asked.

I looked at him, and in that minute, I knew it was really over.

Dylan would never be able to understand. Dylan had been lucky enough to live in a world where everything had been straightforward and safe. He'd never wanted to change who he was, never wanted to try out being someone else. He never stopped pushing for college, which was the goal that he was convinced lay at the end of all of this.

And at one point, that had been me as well. I'd looked at my life and figured out all the steps. If I did what Bristol did, and played a sport and had straight As, never annoyed my parents, dated someone who was just like me and had the same ideas – then one day, I'd wake up and I'd be happy.

But that hadn't happened. Now that Bristol was home, I could see that she'd never been entirely happy either. It had been a mission doomed from the start, because I'd never let myself figure out what it actually was that I wanted. I'd just focused on the goal that I'd always been given.

Our food arrived. I looked at Dylan, who was distracted momentarily by his sandwich and fries. "I think we should break up," I said, feeling a flood of relief as I said the words.

Dylan sat up immediately. "What?" he asked, his mouth full of French fries.

"I think we're in really different places." I shook my head. "I don't want to build my life around what's best for college any more."

"I don't understand," Dylan said, swallowing the French fries he'd been eating and looking at me. "Sutton, we have plans. Are you saying that you don't want to play soccer because you want to try a different sport? Because you can't seriously think that you're going to give up on college."

I looked at him again, seeing the piece of hair that had fallen over his forehead as we'd been talking. The table in between us felt wider than it was, like it had been replaced by a chasm I couldn't cross.

It wasn't that Dylan had changed. It was that I had. "I think that's the difference, Dylan. You know what you want. You want to play lacrosse and focus on college, and those are your plans. I don't know what I want. And I need to figure it out."

Dylan shook his head again. "So you're breaking up with me?" His eyes were slightly widened, his eyebrows bent in what seemed to be confusion.

I took a deep breath, realizing that nothing I said was going to make sense to him. There were so many things changing in my life that I didn't have the words for all of them. "Yes," I replied.

"But we're great together," he said, leaning back in his chair. "We work."

I thought back to Natalie, the way she lit up when she talked about her boy of the moment. I thought about the internship in the cold air-conditioning and lobster ice cream. "I think we used to work. I think I changed."

"Well, this isn't what I was expecting today," Dylan said, his shoulders creeping up around his neck.

"I'm sorry," I said, the words feeling too small for the moment. Sometimes, it was easier to be the one changing than the one left behind. "I'll leave now. Goodbye, Dylan."

He didn't reply, and I took a deep breath and walked up to the counter to pay.

• • •

"OKAY, GIRLS. BLUE OR ORANGE?"

Six hours later, I was over at Natalie's, confronting a dire fashion dilemma. Natalie was standing in front of me and Nora, who were sitting on her bed, a bowl of popcorn in between us. Natalie had one shirt in each hand and was looking at us expectantly, her eyebrows raised.

"This doesn't feel like a decision that requires all of us to vote," Nora replied, sticking her hand into the popcorn bowl again and taking another handful. A few pieces fell into Natalie's blankets.

"Marcus is going to be there tonight, so this is really a critical decision for my future," Natalie replied, waving the shirts towards us again. "Come on, Nora!"

"Oh, that's why this is such a big deal," Nora glanced up. "Marcus."

"The orange shirt isn't going to go well with your hair," I finally said, deciding to take mercy on Natalie. Nora's general strategy seemed to be to not give an answer until Natalie broke down and made the decision herself, which was effective but a little bit cruel.

"Thank you!" Natalie said, throwing her hands up in the air, the shirts flopping around. "See, Nora, that is exactly the kind of constructive feedback I was looking for!"

"You're in for it now," Nora told me, turning over onto her side to look at me more closely. "You're now going to be involved in every small decision and every single overanalysis of anything that Marcus says to her for the rest of time."

"I like to get second opinions sometimes," Natalie called towards us from the closet. "Friends are supposed to be supportive of their friends when they need advice."

"This is why you're lucky to have a boyfriend," Nora said to me. "It saves you from figuring out what some offhand comment actually means and spending all your time overanalyzing things."

"Dylan and I broke up," I said, grabbing a handful of popcorn and stuffing it into my mouth, the last words coming out muffled. "So not any more."

"What?" Natalie demanded, pulling a chair over towards the end of the bed. "You broke up with your boyfriend and weren't going to tell us?"

"It wasn't a big deal," I replied. Once we'd started talking, the inevitable had taken over. I'd known it for a while, now that I thought about it. We'd been drifting apart more and more.

"Hold up," Natalie held up her hand. "Are you sad? Are you happy? What's going on in your brain?"

I paused. The honest answer was nothing – I

didn't feel any different than I had this morning. Maybe it was that Dylan was a small part of everything that was going on in my life, or maybe it was that there just hadn't really been anything there to start with.

The whole process of falling for Dylan had felt a lot like high school – steps I had to check off in order to reach another life milestone. When Dylan had first asked me out, I'd said yes because I had no reason to say no, at least none that I could articulate. And Dylan seemed like he fit all of the boxes that I had laid out for myself. He was popular but not too popular, focused on his future, good grades, but not so good that I would feel inadequate all the time, generically handsome.

Maybe it wasn't fair to say that I had only said yes to Dylan because there were no red flags. Maybe it was more fair to say that I had said yes because Dylan checked off every box on my mental checklist. He had seemed like the right type of guy, and so I had decided that he would be the right boyfriend for me.

Dylan fit into the perfect life package I'd been trying to build for myself, and that had been enough for me then. It was only this summer that I had realized that maybe, I shouldn't have a list. "I think I'm happy," I replied. "I think we just grew apart this summer, and I wanted to go in a different direction than he did."

"That sounds very mature," Nora said. "If you're being that mature now, you're going to tell us later that he actually cheated and was a terrible human. Nobody actually believes this growing apart nonsense."

I laughed. Dylan would never have cheated, if only because it would have interrupted his training schedule. "I don't think he cheated on me. Maybe with lacrosse. That's always been his first love."

"You know what this calls for?" Natalie said, jumping up from her chair.

"Chunky Monkey!" Nora called back, rolling over and standing up from the bed, stretching her arms out.

"What?" I asked, watching Natalie and Nora both start walking towards the door. Natalie elbowed Nora out of the way, starting to run down the stairs. "Where are you going?"

"Come on!" Natalie said, waiting in the doorway until I got up off the bed and started to follow them. "We have a tradition," she explained as we walked down the stairs, "that when one of us has a breakup, we have a pint of Chunky Monkey ice cream together."

"And," Nora added, "the rule is that if you have

walnuts in your spoonful, you have to say something mean about the person you or the other person just broke up with. If you have chocolate chips, you have to say something nice about the person in the room who just went through the breakup. Normally Natalie's the one who gets broken up with, so – "

"Let me remind you, it took us two pints to get through Charles Huntington the Third," Natalie interjected.

"That was because you had so many mean things to say about him that you insisted on getting a second pint out!" Nora replied. "I had a stomachache for days."

"Definitely due to you realizing what a loser you dated, and not related to the ice cream," Natalie replied, reaching into the freezer and digging out a pint. "Sutton, first scoop?"

"Sure," I replied. I wasn't a fan of the flavor, but I'd had much worse this summer. Nora passed me a spoon, and I dug into the ice cream.

"No way. She just got ice cream," Nora said, inspecting my spoon as I pulled it out of the ice cream.

"That can't be possible. This must be a faulty pint," Natalie replied, staring at the spoon. "Say anything you want, I guess."

"I'm glad that I'm doing this here with the two of

you. Thanks for adopting me this summer," I replied, taking a huge bite of ice cream. It was better than I expected, or maybe lobster ice cream made everything delicious in comparison.

Nora looked at me for a second, then gave me a side hug. "I'm going to have to be extra mean to Dylan on the next scoop to make up for all that sincerity, you know."

A pint later, we were back in Natalie's room so that she could put the finishing touches on her outfit. She'd dug out bright colors and sequins from her closet. I felt very bland in a black t-shirt and jean shorts next to her.

"I really wish sequins were more of a thing," Natalie said, turning around to admire her top in the mirror. "Look at me sparkle when I shimmy. It's so snazzy."

"Who uses the word snazzy?" Nora asked, glancing from the bed.

"I do!" Natalie replied. "My top is very snazzy." She shimmed, and I could hear the sequins rattle together ever so slightly. "See? It's the absolute right description for this top."

"This is why English isn't her best subject," Nora said to me.

"I'd like to remind you that you got a C on your

Scarlet Letter paper, while I got an A," Natalie replied.

Nora rolled her eyes at me again. "She's always talking about this. It's the only time she's ever gotten a better grade in English than I have, and she never lets me forget it."

"It's because you don't understand passion properly." Natalie brandished a hairbrush at me. "See, I understand what it's like to fall in love and want to throw everything away for it. Nora just sits here and wonders if the guy will look good on a holiday card with her."

"That is so not true." Nora whipped her head up and crossed her arms, staring at Natalie.

"You said that about Charles Huntington the Third! That's why you liked him!"

Nora sighed. "I said that he would look good on a holiday card, meaning that he was handsome enough to be a stock photo on a website, obviously."

"That doesn't sound like a great compliment. You're saying someone is generic as hell," I replied.

Natalie pointed at me triumphantly with her hair brush. "See! Sutton knows what I'm talking about!"

"Dylan looks like could have belonged on a Christmas card stock photo," I added. I had managed to hold back most of my mean comments about him, but now that I thought of it, it seemed too apt. You could have taken a picture of Dylan with his Labrador Retriever and stuck it into a photo frame, and no one would have ever guessed it wasn't the stock photo.

"Some people are into that," Natalie replied. "I guess you're one of them, Sutton."

"I think I need someone who's less like me, so that they push me more to be different," I replied.

"I don't think that that's necessarily a bad thing, if someone's just like you," Nora replied. "It's easier to have stuff to talk about. It's like having a second half."

"I have so many dirty jokes that I'm not going to make there," Natalie called from her closet, where she was almost completely buried in clothes.

"But what if I don't know what I want my second half to be?" I asked. "I don't know what my first half is supposed to be. I want someone who will help me figure things out."

"Unless they tell you to wear the world's ugliest dress when you go to meet their family, because their parents will just love that sailboat covered puke pink dress that they bought you," Natalie chimed in.

I looked over at Nora. "Seriously? The more stories I hear about Charles, the worse he sounds."

Nora snorted. "I tried to date someone who wasn't just like me. Unfortunately, he was not like me in all of the worst possible ways. There's a reason I don't wear pink."

"But see, that's Sutton's point!" Natalie crawled out of the closet clutching a pair of rhinestone studded sandals. "I knew I had these in there somewhere. But anyway, that's Sutton's point. Charles challenged you to try being someone new. You discovered you didn't like it, and then you went back to what you did before. But now you know that you're not interested in being a pink-pant wearing person for the rest of your life."

"I refuse to accept that this might be a valid point," Nora replied, looking back down at the popcorn bowl. "Any time you use Charles as an example in one of your rants, I just automatically ignore you because you're being ridiculous."

"I usually am," Natalie replied, putting on her shoes, "but that's only because there's so much ridiculous about him that I can't help myself." She stood and shimmed again, the sequins catching the light from her lamp and sending sparkles all around the room. "So are we going to go crush this party, or what?"

This was going to be the party, Natalie had informed us, that satisfied our bucket list item to actually go to a party. "See," she explained in the car as she searched for the perfect pre-party playlist, "we're going out tonight with the objective to just have fun. All three of us are single and ready to mingle."

"That sounds so un-fun that I could puke," Nora replied, looking out the car window.

"It's all a matter of perspective. You should look at it as a limitless opportunity. Who knows what kind of wonderful person you might meet tonight at this party? This could be the night that true love arrives!" Natalie replied, drumming her fingers on the steering wheel.

"I really don't think I'm going to find true love at an Orchards party with warm beer," Nora replied, "but thanks for your boundless optimism."

"Someone in this car has to be an optimist to make up for the rest of you, Eeyore," Natalie replied, then yanked up the volume on what appeared to be the most generic pop music she could find. "Okay, girls, let's get this party started!"

"I hate this song," Nora muttered, slumping down even lower in the back seat.

There were only a few cars at the Orchards when we arrived, and Natalie grabbed a parking spot close to the entrance. "Okay, everyone," Natalie said, taking a deep breath. "We have to be calm and make our entrance fabulous."

"I think it might have helped to wait until people

actually started showing up," Nora replied, looking pointendly around at the empty parking lot.

"Nora, that wasn't the plan," Natalie shook her head, her sequins bouncing again. "I have to be here early so that I can be deep in a fascinating, intellectual conversation when Marcus walks up. I need him to get here and see me looking fresh and alluring, not all sweaty because we had to park a mile away!"

"Oh dear, here we go again," Nora muttered to me as we both stepped out of the car.

The night air was crisper than I had expected given the humidity of the day, and I could hear a few faint murmurs from the people who'd already shown up. Natalie reached into the trunk and passed us all spiked seltzer. "I brought some things to get started. Although if Marcus shows up, I think it'll look better if I have beer with me, so you'll have to grab this from me. I don't want to seem like I'm so high maintenance that I brought my own drinks to the party, you know."

"But you did bring your own drinks to the party," I replied, raising an eyebrow at Natalie.

"See, Sutton, sometimes you have to make sacrifices as you're chasing the loves of your life," Natalie said. "But I don't particularly want that sacrifice to be drinking shitty beer, so I'm compromising."

"She's monologuing, help," Nora mouthed towards me.

"Hey," Stacey said, walking over towards us from her own car. "Great sequins, Natalie."

"Oh, these things?" Natalie asked, pinching her top between two fingers. "I just threw this on before the party. Didn't even think about it."

Stacey grinned at both of us, her eyes lighting up. "Marcus is over by the keg, Natalie."

"Shoot!" Natalie shook her head, throwing her hands up and splashing me with a tiny bit of spiked seltzer. She glanced around and shoved her seltzer into Stacey's hands, who took it without complaint. "I knew we should have left the house earlier!"

"You were the one who took forever trying to figure out what top to put on," Nora grumbled, but she let Natalie lead her away anyway.

"I guessed right with Marcus," Stacey said, taking a sip of her beer and glancing after Natalie and Nora. Nora was literally dragging her feet as she was dragged along into Natalie's latest scheme. "This is a pretty long-lived one. Maybe it'll actually go some-where." She glanced at me. "Last year, Natalie dated someone for six hours. We're not even sure how that worked logistically. My personal theory is that he meant to say something else when he asked her to start dating and was too ashamed to admit it."

"Six hours? How?" It had taken me closer to six weeks to get to the point with Dylan where we thought that we were dating. I couldn't imagine finding someone and then falling for them that quickly.

"You're going out with Dylan Walters, right?" Stacey asked, taking a sip of the spiked seltzer that Natalie had left her and dumping the rest of her beer onto the ground. She glanced. "It tastes awful. Don't judge."

"I'm not. Either judging, or dating Dylan," I replied.

"Really?" Stacey said, turning towards me. "I could have sworn that you and Dylan were together."

"We broke up today," I replied. I almost didn't believe it, hearing myself say it, like there was another Sutton out there. A Sutton who was so confident in herself that she'd just broken up with her boyfriend. She was brave enough to make the big decision.

"I thought there was something going on," Stacey said triumphantly, taking a long slurp of her seltzer and staring at me. "I knew it."

"What are you talking about?" I asked.

"You and Michael, obviously," she replied. "I don't think I've ever seen him around the tennis courts as much as he has been this summer. He doesn't even really like tennis. And when either of you walks into the club, you look around until you see the other person. It's cute, but it's also kind of obvious."

"I like talking to him," I replied. Yes, it was true that I may have looked around for Michael every time I walked into the tennis club. And maybe it was true that I had worn my nicer t-shirts there as opposed to the ones with sweat stains from middle school. But it wasn't just that I liked Michael.

I felt different around him, like I was strangely at peace. Like he'd survived so much worse than I had, and so I could be honest about what I was feeling and he wouldn't judge me. Like I could be myself, even when I didn't know who that was.

Maybe that was what liking someone meant. But it felt like the opposite of Natalie rushing off to meet Marcus, worrying about how her hair looked and whether she had the right friend by her side. Being around Michael felt quiet. The kind of quiet that would come after a giant rainstorm, when the air was fresh and the world felt renewed.

"I'm just telling you this because you are my friend, and Michael is also my friend," Stacey said, glancing sideways at me. The noise of the party suddenly felt much further away than before. "But don't you dare break his heart. Michael is one of my favorite people, and he's already had enough crap happen to him for a lifetime. You be nice."

"Breaking his heart is the last thing I would want to do." There was enough in my life that I would never want to inflict more onto someone else. And especially not Michael.

"Just be careful." Stacey shook her head. "I'm glad you're not dating Dylan Walters any more, because I wouldn't have wanted to be around for the conversation where you explained that to Michael."

Michael didn't know that I was dating Dylan, I realized. I'd never said it to him, because some part of my mind had never wanted to. I glanced back at her, and she suddenly shook her head. "I'm changing the topic," she said in a low voice.

I turned to see Michael standing behind us. "Hey, you two."

"I'm going to get another drink," Stacey said, looking in between the two of us. "And rescue Nora." She waved to Michael and turned around very obviously.

"Rescue Nora?" Michael asked, looking over his shoulder towards where Stacey was walking.

"Natalie is in love. Nora is not happy," I said.

"Is that why Natalie is trying to do a keg stand?" he asked.

I turned and saw that he was unfortunately right.

Marcus was holding Natalie around the middle. None of us had ever seen a keg stand outside of the movies, so I wasn't sure about the logistics. "This party is getting wild," I said.

"You want to leave?" he asked, glancing down at me.

Yes. My brain was screaming at me. "Let's do it." I grabbed my phone and texted my friends.

Michael looked down at me and smiled. "You know, the diner in town will be empty since everyone's at this party. We could get nacho fries."

Sold. French fries covered in cheese and taco beef and salsa and sour cream sounded like the best thing in the world right now. "But you have to get the kind that comes with guac."

Michael laughed and looped his arm around my waist, pulling me next to him. "I think we can make that happen."

Fifteen minutes later, Michael parked in front of the late night diner in town. It offered the weirdest variety of food I'd ever seen in a diner. You could order a full turkey dinner at any time of the year. But most importantly, they had nacho fries.

"My parents stopped letting us get nacho fries after elementary school," I told Michael as we sat down and took our menus. "They think they're not healthy, even though they make my soul happy."

"Cheese is good for protein, and potatoes are good starches," Michael said, resting his arms on the table. "And think of all that avocado in the guacamole."

"Avocados go much better in guac than in ice cream." I shook my head. "Has anyone ever told Brittany's that they should really try making some normal flavors?"

"Like vanilla?" Michael asked, breaking into a grin. His hand started to rest on the table, creeping towards mine in the middle.

I shook my head. "Not that boring. Mint chocolate chip would do."

"I don't think that's a real flavor of ice cream," he replied.

"Oh, shut up," I replied, balling up my napkin to throw at him. As I started to throw it, Michael caught my hand in his, and our eyes locked for a second.

We stayed there for long enough for my stomach to flip. "And, what are you having?" asked the waitress from the other end of the table.

Michael closed his eyes briefly. "One really big order of nacho fries, and a pitcher of water, please."

As the waitress walked away, Michael dropped my hands back onto the table and pushed the water glass in front of me towards me. "Drink up. You can't let yourself get dehydrated when we've got tennis camp this week."

I caught his eyes again, and my stomach flipped. I might have had drinks earlier, but I didn't think that was what was making my stomach have butterflies now.

The waitress arrived with the largest plate of cheese fries I'd ever seen. "Here you go."

This had to be without a doubt the best part of the night. I immediately started to grab the fries, and Michael just sat back and watched me as I ate. "These are the best things I've ever eaten," I let him know as I stuffed another fistful into my mouth.

"I have never seen anyone enjoy any food this much," Michael shook his head.

"I love nacho fries." I took another huge bite. The fries were nicely crispy, not mushy at all. "My two favorite junk foods are nachos and french fries, and this is both of them in one dish."

"I'm glad that I'm here to enable your addiction," Michael said, leaning back in the booth, his eyes never leaving my face. "I don't know what you'd do without those fries."

"Can we just do this instead of going to parties for the rest of the summer?" I asked, the words out of my mouth before I realized how they sounded. I swallowed.

Michael reached across the table again and rested his hand over mine. "I'd like that."

After I'd successfully polished off the entire plate of fries, and Michael had cajoled me into drinking another few glasses of water, we drove back to my house. Michael pulled up to the front door, then stopped the car. "It was great hanging out with you tonight, Sutton."

"It was fun hanging out with you, too," I replied, pausing before I opened the door and got out. "Good night, Michael."

"Good night, Sutton," he replied. I could have sworn that he was about to say something else before he nodded again and drove slowly down the driveway. I paused at the door, watching him drive away.

I walked into the house, navigating carefully through the hallway so that I didn't bump into anything and make a loud noise. I wandered into the kitchen before I turned the lights on, and all of a sudden I heard a shriek.

"What the hell?"

I whipped my head around to see Bristol standing a foot from me. "Sutton, you basically gave me a heart attack," she said, grabbing the counter. "Usually people turn the lights on when they walk into a room, you know."

I looked at her. "You're supposed to be asleep, so stop complaining."

"Oh my god, are you tipsy?" Bristol's face seemed a little too happy for the occasion. "My baby sister has gotten drunk for the first time. This is going to be so much fun."

"I'm not drunk, but I did eat an entire plate of nacho fries. Natalie was though. She was doing a keg stand to impress a guy," I replied.

"You know, getting drunk before talking to someone is not usually the best strategy," Bristol said, cocking her head to the side. "Can definitely be the most fun strategy, but is rarely the best." She paused. "You didn't drive home, did you?"

"I'm not an idiot. Michael drove me home," I replied.

"Michael, that guy who I met at the tennis club last week?" Bristol's eyebrow shot up – just one of them, one of those many mannerisms I'd tried to steal from her when I was younger.

"Yeah, that guy," I replied. "We left and got fries together. I wasn't feeling drinking at a party."

"Oh, I totally approve of this guy. Those nacho fries are the absolute best," Bristol replied, grabbing a kitchen stool and sitting down. "Wait, aren't you dating Dylan Walters?"

"Was," I replied. "I broke up with him today."

"Oh thank god. He seemed like he had the personality of a bag of flour," Bristol replied. She glanced at me, then got up, went to the fridge, and passed me a bottle of something. She tapped her foot on the floor, then looked at me expectantly. "So are you dating this Michael guy?"

"No. I'm not sure what we are," I said, looking at Bristol. "He's great. He's the kind of person I can spend hours just hanging out with. And he's smart and thoughtful, and he even puts up with the kids at camp."

Bristol looked at me. "I think you know what you want, Sutton."

"I SURVIVED!" Natalie yelled towards the sky.

Nora and I were both lying on the tennis courts on our backs after our most intense day of camp yet. It had been raining for the past several days, which meant that the kids had a lot of energy to burn off today.

"I don't want to do this any more," Nora said, still lying on the ground. "I have bruises from the number of tennis balls that were thrown at me today."

"No one attempted to grab your hair to see if they could rub the pink off," Natalie replied. "I got the worst day award."

"We had a 'whack Sutton with a tennis ball' game," I replied. "I think we all had equally awful days."

"This is very true," Nora groaned again, rolling over onto her side. "Why do we do this?"

"Because secretly we love these little jerks?" Natalie asked. "Even when they grab my hair and try to rub out the color."

I laughed. "I'm actually starting to really like the little jerks." Today, one of the boys had told me that I was his favorite tennis coach ever, which had secretly made me thrilled, although I wasn't going to tell the rest of them that. And he'd followed it up by throwing a ball at my head, which had ruined the sentiment somewhat.

"Ugh. I should get home," Nora said, pushing herself off the ground. I nodded and followed her, waving as we headed out towards our cars.

I reached into my car and pulled my phone out of my bag. I had a text from Michael. *How was your day at tennis camp? Secretly glad this was my day off*

Oh, it was awful. It was completely awful but also wonderful, I texted back. *I have so many bruises from having tennis balls being thrown at me. You own all of us one for skipping today*

I'll make it up to you, I promise, he texted back, followed by a smiley emoji. Interesting. I'd never seen Michael use an emoji before. He definitely didn't seem like an emoji kind of person.

I drove home, looking forward to my shower. I was disgustingly sweaty, the kind of sweaty where you wanted to jump in the nearest river. I parked and walked into the house, rolling my shoulders. Finally having a shower after being out in the sun chasing kids all day sounded amazing.

"Sutton?" My mom was standing at the kitchen counter, my dad next to her rummaging through the fridge. "Where have you been? I called your office this morning because you weren't answering your phone. They told me that you'd resigned from your internship two weeks ago."

Oh, shit. This was not good. I should have never put off telling them. It was going to be ten times worse now. "Yeah. I quit."

That was my dad's cue to turn around from the fridge. "Sutton, we're confused," he said, leaning against the counter and facing me. "You had a good internship opportunity, and you quit without telling us. This is extremely concerning."

"I didn't quit my internship to play tennis." None of what I was doing was playing around. It was a hard job. "I coach kids. It's a job too. It's not like I'm slacking off."

"But you're not following through on your

commitments," my mom said, stepping sideways so that she and my dad formed a solid block. "These types of things could have a really negative impact on your college applications. This doesn't seem like you."

But that was the problem. It *was* me. I swallowed, forcing my voice to stay level. "I'm not doing this because I think it's good for college. I'm doing what I want to do, and I'll figure the college piece out when I get there."

"Sutton, it doesn't seem like you understand the severity of this," my dad replied. Clearly he was going to be a bad cop in this situation. "You can't just leave things that you don't want to do and not follow through on your commitments. Maturity is sticking to what you promised, not quitting midway through because you've decided you'd rather goof off."

Was he kidding? Did he have any idea how hard it was to keep a bunch of eight year olds from hitting each other with rackets? "Goof off? Seriously?" I took a step towards the counter. "I'm not goofing off. I still have an actual job. Rather than sitting in that room scanning things, I'm working with kids, and I like it!"

My parents exchanged a look, and my mom cleared her throat. "I think we're concerned about where this recent behavior is coming from, Sutton. I met the Walters at the grocery store today. I was very surprised to hear that you had broken up with Dylan. It came completely out of the blue for him."

Maybe if he'd bothered to text me from his lacrosse camp, it wouldn't have been so out of the blue for him. I took a deep breath. "It shouldn't have been. He didn't call me for weeks because he was so focused on his stupid lacrosse camp."

"You broke up with Dylan, and you've failed to honor your commitments to your internship and this family." My mom shook her head, then glanced at my dad. Of course. She was bringing him in for the bad news.

"We don't know where this behavior is coming from, but it's completely unacceptable. You're banned from working at that tennis camp for the rest of the summer, and you will apologize to Bethany and honor your commitments to her," my dad finished for her.

They couldn't take away tennis camp from me. "So you're going to stand here and yell at me about honoring commitments, and now you want me to call up somewhere I've committed to and tell them that I can't make it? Great idea, Dad."

"Sutton!" My dad hit the counter with the flat of his hand. "That tone is not appreciated."

"We're just concerned about what's been going on with you, Sutton. This behavior is new, and we want to be sure that we address it now before it impacts your college applications," my mom said.

I stared at my parents for a second. "Are you serious?" With everything that happened this summer, we were going to worry about college applications?

My parents looked at each other, and I took a deep breath. I couldn't keep talking, couldn't say any more, or I'd say things that I couldn't take back. I took another breath and then turned and left the kitchen, leaving my parents standing there at the counter.

I walked upstairs and into the shower. I paced around the shower, taking gulps of water and air at the same time, trying to bring my heart rate back down. My parents couldn't honestly believe that this was all because of tennis camp.

I didn't know how to explain any of this to them. I didn't know how to say that we'd never talked about Bristol. It was like we couldn't admit to ourselves that things had changed.

It was a good thing that we were changing. We all needed to change, and now that I'd seen what happened to Bristol when she didn't change, I knew that I needed it. I knew that I didn't know who I was, but I liked this Sutton a whole lot more.

I turned off the shower, not even sure if I'd gotten all the shampoo out of my hair. I dried off, pulled on my clothes, and walked down the hall towards Bristol's room.

I stood next to the door for a minute, not sure what I was waiting for. I could have knocked, but I didn't know what I was going to say. I started to hear Bristol's laugh and Mia's voice, and realized she was on the phone. I walked back into my room, lying back on my bed and staring at the ceiling.

A WEEK LATER, I walked downstairs to find something to eat.

My parents had not been kidding about forbidding me to go to tennis. I was allowed out of the house to go to the gym each day, but only if my dad accompanied me. I wasn't sure if he expected that I'd run away from the gym, or if it was my mom's way of forcing him to go as well.

When I got home from the gym, my mom supervised me while I renamed files for Bethany. This was my summer now.

It was strange to me that two months ago, I would have been happy with this. I would have told myself it was a good way to prepare for the fall. But now, all I wanted to do was to see Natalie and Nora. And Michael.

My phone buzzed again as I walked down the

steps, and I pulled it out to see another text on the group thread, a photo of Natalie and Nora out at ice cream, grinning at the camera. *Sutton, we miss you!*

Natalie: *I could totally break you out of house arrest. I've watched enough true crime on Netflix to know how*

Nora: *Sutton, please don't encourage her*

I tucked the phone back in my pocket. Even the texts made my heart hurt, knowing that there was so much that I was missing. We still hadn't finished the bucket list, but at least Natalie had stopped telling me about the pants, clearly sensing it would make the fear of missing out worse.

My parents were in the kitchen, standing at the doorway, when I reached the bottom of the stairs. "Sutton." I hated the way my dad said my name now, tinged with disappointment.

"Yeah?" I asked, turning towards the fridge. They were going to

"Your mom and I are going to be heading out today and will be away for the night. We have a meeting in the city that we can't put off any longer," my dad said.

"Don't think about doing anything," my mom said, as though she knew where my thoughts were going. "You are still grounded."

As though I could have forgotten that. "I know. Have a good trip."

They smiled towards me, then turned to go out the door. They'd still hidden my keys. I'd never had them not trust me before.

As their car pulled out of the driveway, Bristol poked her head around the corner. "They're gone?"

"Yeah," I said, sitting down at the counter.

My phone buzzed again. Natalie: *Sutton. Tonight is the opportunity. And you know what I mean, but I can't write it out, because larceny.*

Nora: *You know, it doesn't really cover up crimes to write "I can't say what I'm doing because it is a crime."*

Natalie: *It is a service to humanity, Nora.*

I snorted. That stupid bucket list was coming to mean so much more than it ever would have at the beginning of the summer. I was scared of doing it, and now I'd done it all.

"Something funny?" Bristol asked, nodding towards my phone.

I pushed my phone aside. "Natalie and Nora have a summer bucket list, and we're trying to cross off the last item. We're stealing some pants."

Bristol looked at me for a second, then nodded. "Look, do what you have to do."

I was lucky that my sister was so cool about so

many things. But suddenly, something blossomed in the back of my head. If anyone knew about sneaking out, it was Bristol. "I really hate to ask you this."

"Great opening," she said, sitting down on the kitchen stool next to mine.

"I know." I swallowed. "I really want to finish this bucket list. I mean, I ate lobster bisque ice cream. I can't miss this."

Bristol's mouth started to quirk up into a grin. "And you are going to tell me that you need me to cover for you."

"Is that too much to ask?" I'd never asked her to do something for me before, and now I was asking her to break the rules.

She swiveled her chair towards the window. "Okay. So you're going to want to leave through the backyard. Act like you're going to the oak tree back there, then make a hard turn behind it. There's a dead zone for the back door camera."

"You've snuck out before?" I asked. Bristol was supposed to be too rule abiding for that.

She laughed. "Of course I snuck out in high school. Leave your phone here with me. I'll move it around the house in case Mom and Dad are checking find my friends. And make sure your friends text me a picture of these pants."

I reached over and gave her the biggest hug. "Bristol, you're the best."

"Go get in running clothes just in case anyone spots you." She grinned. "God, my sister is finally becoming cool."

I started to jog upstairs. I could totally run over to Stacey's in time. It wouldn't be fun, but I could do it.

I stopped. There was one item on the bucket list that I hadn't thought about. *Sneak out of the house, ideally to meet a boy.*

Well then. I picked up my phone and started a new text. *Can you come get me?*

I WALKED through the backyard and around the house, following Bristol's directions. I snuck across the neighbor's backyard, then peeled off and ran towards the street.

Michael was sitting in his car, and he shook his head as I grabbed the door handle and threw myself in. My heart was pounding.

"Should I just drop you off at Stacey's?" Michael asked, leaning towards me a second and then pulling back. His eyes stared at mine, and I swallowed. "What are you doing?"

I had to explain this without being too weird.

"Have you heard about Charles Huntington the Third?" I asked.

"I've met him, and he is insufferable," Michael replied. "He opened a conversation with me by telling me about his boat."

"That sounds about right. I didn't think that Natalie was capable of hating anyone, but she hates him. And we're going to steal his pants for revenge," I said as Connor started to drive.

"That's weird, but I approve," Michael replied. "As long as you're not violent."

"Again, if there's anyone who deserves it, it would be Charles Huntington the Third," I replied.

"Well, I expect to see a picture of these pants later," Michael replied. He glanced over at me. "It's weird your parents still haven't given you your keys back."

"It was the biggest fight I've had with them, ever," I replied. "They were worried about me quitting my internship and breaking up with Dylan, and – "

"Quitting your internship and what?"

Oh. "I broke up with Dylan Walters. We'd been going out for a few months, and it wasn't working, but my parents really liked him." I glanced over at Michael, who seemed to be staring at the road more intensely than required. "But it's over now."

"I didn't know you were going out with some-one," Michael replied. His hands tightened, then loosed on the steering wheel.

"Not any more," I said again.

Michael nodded, still staring at the road ahead of us. I tried to catch his eye, even for a second "That's good then," Michael replied slowly. "As long as you're happier."

"I think I figured out what was important, and I shouldn't have stayed for so long," I said. *I realized he wasn't you,* I wanted to say, but I didn't have the courage.

We pulled up in front of Stacey's driveway. "I hope everything's okay," Michael said, stopping in front of Stacey's and looking directly at me.

I caught his eyes and my heart flipped again. "Maybe not right now, but it will be soon."

"TELL ME THE TRUTH," Stacey demanded as she microwaved dinner leftovers for me. "What's going on with you and Michael?"

"I had a fight with my parents, and they have my car keys," I replied. "He was nice enough to pick me up and drive me over here."

"That is not the question I'm asking, and you

know it," Stacey replied, shaking her head. "You like him, don't you."

It didn't even feel like a question at this point. "I do. But I just don't know how to say it. I just stopped dating Dylan, and I don't want to just rebound onto Michael," I said as she passed me food.

"No offense, but your relationship with Dylan never particularly seemed like it was much of a relationship," Stacey replied.

"It wasn't." Sitting here now, I could see that.The idea of talking to Dylan about the things I talked to Stacey and Michael about was just absurd. He'd been lucky enough that nothing had ever knocked him off his life plan, and it was like he couldn't understand what that was.

Someday, something would happen and he'd figure it out. But I couldn't wait around for that to happen.

"So what's the hesitation about telling Michael?" she asked, passing me a seltzer as she waited for the microwave.

"Other than you threatening me if I break his heart?" I said.

"I'm threatening you because I care about you, and I care about him. It kills me to watch you guys just tiptoeing around it. I can't deal with having the two of you sending any more sideways glances at tennis," Stacey replied, then shook her head. "Although if you do start dating, there's a strict no-PDA rule at tennis camp. We cannot horrify the children."

"The children you're talking about threatened to punch Michael in the balls to see if it hurt," I replied.

"I'm not saying they're good children, but I am saying that we have to protect their innocence," Stacey replied, grinning and sliding the now warm leftovers across the table towards me. "Eat up. I'm going to go find you some properly colored clothing."

An hour later, Stacey and I pulled up to Natalie's. Natalie walked outside wearing a catsuit and a ski mask.

"I am not getting involved in this if we're going to rob a bank or something," Stacey replied, raising her eyebrows at Natalie. "This was not supposed to get us arrested."

"Look, girls, we have a plan," Natalie replied, dramatically whipping out a piece of paper.

"Normally people don't write their great robbery plans on Lisa Frank stationary they found in their elementary school binders," Nora replied. She was wearing a black t-shirt and dark jeans, but fortunately had skipped the ski mask.

"I stalked Charles on Instagram," Natalie started.

"Oh god," Nora said, closing her eyes.

"Don't worry, I made a burner account so that no one knows," Natalie replied.

"You made a what?" Stacey's eyebrows shot up.

"I made a burner account. See?" Natalie passed her phone to me, and I saw a boats_and_isalnd_breeze account populated with stock photos of boats. "I followed Charles, and he immediately accepted my follow request. It's like he actually wants people to know how lame he is."

"I hate everything," Nora muttered, covering her face with her hands.

"Anyway, I used the burner account to watch his Instagram stories," Natalie said, flipping her hand out at Nora. "Tonight, he's going to the beach with a bunch of other super lame people from school. But, I did figure something else out."

"How much internet stalking did you do?" Stacey asked.

"I have priorities," Natalie replied. She tapped her phone on the car seat, whipping around to face me and Nora in the backseat. "So here's the thing. Charles Huntington the Third has been following Emily Zhao."

"I think I follow Emily," I said. We had had a bunch of classes together the year before, and she seemed cool. "What's your point?"

"No, Charles Huntington the Third has been

really following Emily Zhao," Natalie replied. "He likes every single one of her pictures, and he usually leaves comments. She comments back sometimes."

"This is getting to a new level of creepy," Stacey replied. "Both Charles commenting on Emily, and your stalking."

"And," Natalie said dramatically, ignoring Stacey, "Emily Zhao posted today that she's daring everyone tonight to swim out to the rock in the harbor with her. And you know that Charles likes her, so you know what he's going to do?"

"He's going to go swimming to impress Emily," I replied.

"Exactly." Natalie nodded. "And as much as he loves those awful pants, he can't go swimming in them without Emily thinking he's a total loser. So what he'll end up doing is taking off his pants and leaving them on shore somewhere."

"So we're going to take his pants while he's swimming and leave him to go back to the party pantsless?" I asked. The scribbles on the Lisa Frank stationary were starting to make sense.

"Exactly," Natalie nodded. "Brilliant, foolproof plan. Stacey, let's drive."

We pulled up to the town beach twenty minutes later. Nora had sunk down in her seat as far as she could. "I cannot believe I'm getting pulled into this."

"Okay, girls, in position," Natalie said, pulling her ski mask down over her eyes.

"Natalie, you really look like you're going to rob a bank. I don't think the ski mask is necessary."

"Oh, it is," Natalie replied. "See, the issue we have is that Charles knows me, and he obviously unfortunately knows Nora. So Sutton, we've nominated you and Stacey to go to the party and steal the pants. Stacey will be the guard at the party, and Sutton, you'll be the pants thief."

"Me?" This was quickly becoming much more than I bargained for. "No way. I'm not cut out to be a thief."

"Everyone needs to try something new at some point in their life, right?" Natalie asked. "That's the whole point of the summer bucket list."

Stacey turned around in the driver's seat and looked back at me. "That is the point of the bucket list, Sutton."

"You're just saying that so that you don't have to be the pants thief!" I protested.

"Look, Nora had to date the guy. That was much worse," Natalie cut us off. "Okay. I'm going to be the lookout at the car, so if we need to relay the pants, we can. And then Nora will sit here in the driver's seat and be our getaway vehicle."

"Do we need a getaway vehicle?" Stacey asked, looking down at the list.

"You see? I've thought of everything," Natalie replied triumphantly, although her words were slightly muffled by the ski mask over her face. "Okay, girls. Let's get in position."

"This is officially the most ridiculous thing that I've ever done," Stacey told me as we walked towards the gathering of people on the beach.

"You're not wearing a ski mask and a catsuit in the middle of the summer," I replied

"Hey, Stacey!" Emily called as we walked onto the beach. "I didn't know that you were coming."

"Last minute," Stacey replied. I heard that something was going on tonight, and I was getting bored at home, you know?"

"You didn't bring a bathing suit, by chance?" Emily asked. "I challenged a bunch of people to a race out to the rock, but I was hoping that a few of us could beat them."

"No, unfortunately," Stacey replied, shaking her head.

"Too bad." Emily leaned towards us. "You know Charles Huntington? He's been constantly telling me what a great swimmer he is, so I challenged him to a swim contest tonight."

"That does sound like a good cause," I replied.

"Sutton, right?" Emily said, turning towards me. "Hi. I'm happy you made it out, too. You should have hung out more with us last year."

It didn't sound like a reproach so much as a fact. Emily had been in the friend group that I'd drifted out of sophomore year, and one of those people who I'd always really liked from a distance. "I'm going to be better this year," I promised. "It'll be the best senior year of our lives."

Emily grinned and gave me a fist bump. "You've got it."

Stacey and I waved to her as she headed over to another group of people, then stared at each other. "So what are we supposed to do here?" I asked.

"I guess just hang out and look non-suspicious until Emily challenges Charles to a swim race," Stacey replied. "I'm so glad that she's doing this."

"I'm still slightly weirded out by the fact that Natalie went that deep on internet stalking," I said.

"I don't think there's anyone who can stop Natalie once she puts her mind to something," Stacey replied.

We stood there for a few more minutes, the breeze from the water pushing my hair back slightly. It was nice, standing here next to the beach. Across the beach, I heard cheering, and Stacey poked me in the side. "Let's get moving."

Stacey weaved through the crowd towards Emily. Charles had walked over to Emily and was in the middle of saying something. I glanced over, trying to understand what was going on when I was too far away to hear.

Nora's phone buzzed in my pocket. A text from Stacey – *Men's bathroom.*

I glanced over my shoulder and then headed to behind the men's bathroom. I crouched down behind the building, trying to peer around the side.

"Can't believe you're actually going to do this, man," I heard a voice.

It was followed by another voice, just whiny enough that I knew it had to be Charles Huntington the Third. "Emily dared me to. I'm obviously going to do it. She'll have no respect for me if I can't swim faster than she can to that rock."

I was pretty sure that Emily was the second fastest swimmer on the school swim team, but that hadn't occurred to him.

"I'm getting changed," I heard. I lay down on the ground. I should be inconspicuous enough behind the bathroom building and the bushes that no one would notice me. Hopefully.

I heard noise from inside the bathroom and waited, then waited some more.

Text from Stacey – *everyone's out of the bath-*

room. Go time

I peered around the side of the building to see a group of boys in their swim trunks heading towards the beach. Charles Huntington was wearing a Speedo, which was overkill.

I crept around the front of the building and walked into the bathroom. There were clothes all over the floor, and I glanced around. How was I supposed to tell which one was Charles?

I heard footsteps behind me and sprinted into the bathroom stall. I locked the door and pulled my feet up so no one could see me.

There was a loud burp and the sound of someone taking off their belt outside the bathroom stall. Ew.

I covered my ears, then I heard footsteps leaving the bathroom. Wait. Had that guy not washed his hands? Boys were so gross.

I peered through the crack in the stall door. No one there. I crept out of the stall, glancing around the room. My eyes caught on something brightly colored.

How had I missed these? There were pants with giant colored triangles – pink and green and yellow – overlaid with tiny embroidered sailboats. These were truly the ugliest pants that I had ever seen.

I reached into the pocket and pulled out a wallet. Charles Huntington's school ID was on the top. Bingo.

I glanced at the pants for a second. I took out his phone and wallet, laying them all back down where the pants had been.

I couldn't take his wallet. That was stealing. The pants were a public service trash removal.

Phone again. *They're on their way back from the rock!! Hurry!!*

I grabbed the pants and started to run, my heart hammering.

On the beach, the first person got out of the water. I sprinted towards the car, hugging the pants to my chest.

A figure dressed all in black ran out from beside me, grabbing the pants. It was Natalie. "Run!" she screamed, taking off towards the car.

I took a deep breath, then started to slowly walk back towards the party from the direction of the women's bathroom. I could act like this was normal, and I'd just gone to the bathroom myself. I took a deep breath. Just as long as I didn't seem too stressed.

"You always take forever to pee," Stacey said, raising an eyebrow at me as I walked up next to her, still trying to get my breathing fully under control. She glanced around, then said under her breath, "Don't worry. Nobody noticed that you were gone."

Was that a good thing? But before I could think

about it, Emily walked up to us. "Guess who won?" she crowed, throwing her hands up in the air.

"Not fair, you didn't tell us it was a butterfly," one of the guys behind her moaned. "That's the hardest stroke."

I was pretty sure it was also the stroke where Emily held the school record. "You're just a sore loser," Emily replied.

Stacey gave Emily a high-five. "I think we're going to head out, but that was amazing," she said.

Emily laughed and grinned at us. "'I'm glad you two were here to see it. I hope this goes down in history as the time that a couple of jerks decided to brag too much and got what they had coming."

"Oh, they definitely did," Stacey said, giving me a smile. "Nice work."

We walked back to the car, where Natalie and Nora were waiting. Natalie had taken off her ski mask and crossed her arms over her chest. "There's no point having a getaway car if you're going to take your sweet time getting back here," Nora grumbled.

"If we had booked it out of there, everyone would have known that we were up to something," Stacey replied, getting in the passenger seat and buckling her seatbelt. "So who's ready for our celebratory ice cream?"

· · ·

"THESE REALLY ARE the world's ugliest pants," Stacey said, holding them up as we ate our ice cream. No one had texted us about missing pants, so we were safe and out of the danger zone.

More importantly, I'd found the last flavor I needed to complete my summer challenge, mint chocolate chip. Nora glanced over at me and pretended to gag.

"I can't believe you ever dated someone like that," Natalie said, looking from Nora to the pants and back again.

"It's not my fault. Love makes you blind," Nora replied. "I can see now why those pants should have been a red flag."

"They aren't just a red flag, they're a green, yellow, pink, and sailboat covered flag," Natalie continued, hoisting the pants into the air.

"Are you saying that Marcus would never wear such pants?" Stacey asked, raising an eyebrow.

"Marcus wears jeans and t-shirts all the time, and that is fantastic," Natalie replied. "Doesn't he look great in jeans? He looks great in jeans," she continued.

"You know, Sutton, I'm glad that you joined us at camp this summer," Nora said, cutting off Natalie's monologue. "I wasn't expecting you to be down for pants stealing."

I looked at the three of them again, at the bizarre ice cream flavors we were eating, at the pink pants glowing in summer light. "I'm glad I found you too."

"BRISTOL?" I asked, pressing Stacey's phone up to my ear. "Is it okay if I stay out tonight? I mean, can you cover for me?"

Stacey had volunteered her house for a sleepover. Since Natalie's younger brother was learning the drums, that was a relief.

"Of course I will cover for you." I heard the fridge open in the background. "But you have to bring me ice cream on the way back. We're out."

"I can definitely do that. I promise I'll even get you a normal flavor and not the lobster," I replied.

"And why haven't I gotten a picture of these pants yet?" she asked, the noise of the fridge closing in the background.

That was honestly the most important question. "I'll send one. I promise."

"Okay. Love you," she said.

"Love you too," I replied automatically as we pulled into Stacey's driveway.

"I'm going to shower," Natalie announced once we arrived back at Stacey's. "I'm so sweaty."

"Generally, you sweat a lot when you decide to

wear a ski mask and a catsuit in the middle of the summer," Nora said.

"I was properly dressed for the occasion. Even if someone had caught me running with the pants, they wouldn't have had any idea who I was," Natalie replied. "It was a foolproof plan, and I'm really not sure why you can't see it that way."

Nora rolled her eyes at me. "Do you see what I have to put up with?"

"Keep talking, and I'm going to dye your hair pink in your sleep," Natalie called back.

I glanced out the kitchen window, where I could see another house, a single light still on downstairs. "Stacey, I'm going to go do something really fast," I said.

Stacey raised an eyebrow. Nora crossed her arms and stared at me, clearly waiting for me to trip up under pressure and say more than I meant. She wasn't getting me this time. "I'll be back in a few minutes," I said, walking towards the door.

I paused at the doorway and saw the pants crumpled on the floor next to me. I reached down and picked them up, then tucked them under my arm as I went outside. I rang the doorbell at the house next door, standing out, holding a pair of the most ridiculous pants in the world.

"Sutton?" Michael came to the door. He was

wearing a pair of gray running shorts and a t-shirt, looking like he'd just gotten up from the couch. "Is everything okay?"

I held up the pants towards him. "You told me to send you a picture of Charles Huntington the Third's pants once we successfully stole them. But it's even better to see them in person."

Michael looked at me, his gaze lingering a second too long on my face, and then down at the pants. "Wow. Yeah. Those are awful pants." He paused. "Do you want to come in?"

"Um, yeah," I said, still holding the pants as I followed Michael into his house.

"So, um, can I get you something to drink?" Michael asked, glancing from my face down to the pants I was still holding. "Or did you just want to come over to show me those pants?"

I took a deep breath and looked up at him. He was handsome under the kitchen lights, looking somehow older and wiser than I'd ever imagined him. "I lied earlier."

"What?" Michael asked, pulling out the kitchen stool next to me and sitting down. "What do you mean?"

"I lied," I said again, pulling in another gulp of air. "When I told you why I broke up with Dylan. Maybe it wasn't a lie, but it was only half the truth."

Michael put his hand on the counter next to mine, but didn't say anything, his eyes traveling over my face. "I broke up with Dylan because he wasn't right for me, but the reason that I knew that is because I like you." I gulped, looking down at the counter rather than at Michael's face. "Because I feel about you what I never felt about Dylan, and I realized that being with Dylan was wrong."

Michael seemed frozen in place for a second, and my heart lurched. I could have read everything wrong. Stacey could have read everything wrong. I could be throwing away what we had by admitting this.

Without saying anything, he covered my hand on the counter with his. "I like you, too, Sutton," he said finally, breaking into a smile. "I'm glad you're not dating Dylan any more."

"So do you think there's a chance for us?" I asked, my heart racing, feeling his hand tighten around mine.

He grinned back at me. "I think there's a really good chance for us."

He stood up and pulled me into a hug. I could feel his steady, deep heartbeat as I rested my head on his chest. "This wasn't the summer I was expecting," Michael said, his head resting on top of mine, "but I'm very glad it turned out this way."

TEN

Shockingly, my parents didn't seem to notice the change the next day when they came back from their trip. I felt like my whole body was buzzing with possibility. Michael and I were together. I had the best friends that I could ask for.

Finishing the bucket list hadn't been an ending but a beginning.

Bristol had given me a high five when Stacey dropped me off the next morning. "Success?"

I had just nodded, unable to even make the right words. "Success."

Suddenly, everything in the house reminded me of Michael. Even if I technically wasn't allowed to leave to go to camp or to visit anyone, my parents couldn't stop me from texting him. *Missing my training partner today,* he texted me, sending me a picture of the tennis court.

I was about to text him back when I decided to actually call him. He was my boyfriend now, wasn't he? And I could do that.

God, even thinking those words sent a wave of happiness through me. It had never been like this with Dylan.

"Hey," Michael said, immediately picking up on the other end.

"I wish that I was at tennis, too." The words felt so much stronger now that I was finally saying them out loud.

"We'll convince your parents at some point that they have to let you off house arrest." *We.* It was such a simple word, but there was so much promise in it. *We'd* finish the bucket list, *we'd* help me with my parents.

"It's going to be a while." School would start up again before my parents would relent. I was sure of it. They were set on the idea that Bristol and I were just suffering from a lack of structure.

"Are you coming to the thing tonight?" he asked, and in the background, I could hear shouting his name. It sounded like Stacey, and my heart compressed again, missing them both.

"What thing?" I asked.

"My dad's memorial fund party." The words came out so easily from him that I almost missed it.

I had totally forgotten about that. After Coach Shipman had died, a few of the parents in the youth program had set up a fund in his memory. I wasn't sure what the fund actually did, but it was something for charity and youth sports.

And of course my parents were donors to it, and of course we'd go to the event that was raising money. I would have dreaded another family event, but Michael was going to be there. "Yeah. I'll be there."

For a second, I wondered if I sounded too excited, but there was something about Michael that made me not worry as much. I knew that he was going to be there, even if I was too excited about something, even if I said something stupid.

I didn't have to think about those things, because I knew that he was going to look beyond that. Maybe it wasn't butterflies, but it was just comfort, the sense of coming home.

"Awesome." Maybe now I was reading into it, but he sounded excited too.

In the background, I could hear Stacey calling his name again. "I think you might want to go help her before she gets attacked by angry parents," I said.

Stacey must have forgotten her own rule and not told the children to hydrate, and now there was a mob after her.

He laughed. "She kicked Alex out of the program for next summer after he attacked Nora with a racket one too many times. His parents are furious."

How Stacey managed to put up with this was beyond me. "Go protect her. I'll see you tonight."

"See you tonight," he replied, hanging up on the phone. I stood there for a second, holding the phone in my hands and feeling its warmth.

EIGHT HOURS LATER, I was in the backseat of my parents' car, Bristol next to me. She hadn't wanted to come to anything, but my parents had won that argument, of course. There was a limit to what we could do when they had the car keys.

I glanced over at her. She was staring out the window. I reached over and squeezed her hand, like I'd done back when we were kids. She turned for a second, giving me a smile.

We pulled into the parking lot of one of the local restaurants, and my mom turned back towards us. "Isn't this exciting?"

Considering that the last time we'd done something as a family, it had turned out with me having to find Mia at Starbucks, I didn't think so. But I would take any excuse to see Michael. I nodded.

There were already people wandering around the front of the restaurant. We got out of the car. Bristol glanced over her shoulder, then took a step closer to me. "These people," she muttered under her breath.

"Sutton!" Michael walked straight up towards me, a giant smile on his face. "You made it."

Bristol looked at me, flicking her eyes from Michael to me and back again. "Hi, Michael." She was absolutely going to make fun of me later. I knew it was coming.

"Hey, Bristol," he said, letting his hand brush across the small of my back. I wanted to turn and lean totally into him, but stopped myself. Bristol would make too much fun of me. "I didn't know that you were coming."

She shrugged. "My parents wanted me to come. But I'm happy that I came out. Your dad was a good dude."

"He was," Michael said, nodding. "And I think he liked coaching you, even if you were kind of a jerk to him."

Bristol snorted. "Kind of?"

Michael looked at me, his eyes softening again. "Did you know that your sister once hurtled a lacrosse ball through a window because she was furious about something?"

That didn't sound like Bristol. Bristol had things under control. "We kick kids out of tennis camp for that, Bristol," I said, turning towards her.

She laughed again. "Sutton, I think you might have thought that I was a better person than I actually was."

There were so many layers to that statement that I didn't know where to begin. I nodded. "Clearly I did."

Michael glanced towards the front of the room, then back at us. "I have to go and see my mom, but sit with me later, okay?"

"Yeah!" My voice was definitely too excited, but I could be awkward and excited. I didn't have to pretend.

Bristol poked me in the side as soon as Michael walked away. "This is hilarious to me. You and Michael Shipman."

"What's funny about it?" God, I was definitely smiling so much that my face was going to hurt.

"It's just funny." She snorted. "You know that I remember him as being the little kid at practice who was whining all the time."

"I'm not that much younger than you are." Bristol always seemed to forget that, just because she was in college and I wasn't. Something about going to college aged people ten years overnight in their own minds.

"I know, but those few years make all the difference." She gazed out over my head at the assembled people.

My parents had vanished into the crowd, and I looked at Bristol. "Should we find snacks?"

She nodded. "Snacks seem like a good idea. I wouldn't mind having something to eat before we have to sit through all of this."

"Why did you come if you don't want to sit through all of this?" Bristol wasn't the person who did things just because people asked her to. Not any more.

"I really, really respect Coach Shipman. I don't want to be here at all, but I will deal with it because it's for a person who I cared about and who meant a lot to me." She looked at me and then grinned. "And I wanted to see how red you turned when Michael walked up to you."

My sister was the worst sometimes. I loved her, but she sucked. "Fine then."

We walked towards the snacks table, and I

glanced over my shoulder. "Oh no," Bristol said, watching a person starting to walk over towards us.

It was a couple of very tall people, and I stared at them for a second. Bristol's high school lacrosse coach. "Bristol!" His voice boomed over us. "You're here!"

Bristol's eyes widened, and she took a step back. "What are you doing? How are you doing? Is your leg starting to feel better? You're going to be back at Dartmouth in the fall, right?"

Bristol's breathing sped up, and I looked at her. Something felt wrong. "Bristol!" Someone else was walking up now, a woman in a fashionable dress. "So you decided to come and speak after all!"

"Speak?" I turned towards Bristol, who was standing there.

"Bristol is going to be giving a tribute to Coach Shipman!" I still didn't know who this woman was, just that she looked like every other mother in the neighborhood.

"No, I'm not," Bristol said quickly, looking from me to the woman again.

"Your parents confirmed it at the beginning of the summer," she replied, not noticing the way Bristol was looking at me. "It's a key part of our program."

I would fix this. I didn't know how, but I was going to fix it. "I'm handling it," I said, forcing the biggest smile that I could.

The woman stared at me for a second, and I stepped in front of Bristol. "We'll be starting in half an hour. It's very important to us that Bristol speaks."

"I need to go," Bristol choked out, turning and starting to walk away. She couldn't run, not right now. Not with her leg.

The woman stared at me, her eyes narrowing. I had to say something, get them away so I could get Bristol. "Her ACL." It was the first thing that I could think of, even if it felt wrong to lie again.

But that was what her coaches wanted to hear, apparently. That everything was just her leg, and that was the end of the story. They nodded. "Of course," the woman said, her voice suddenly dropping down to a confidential whisper. "We can make sure to have a chair for her up on stage. We can't have her standing for too long if she's struggling with recovery."

I didn't even have the time to think about those words, struggling with recovery, before I turned and almost ran after her. "Bristol?" I turned down a hallway towards where the caterers had set up in the back. "Are you okay?"

She was leaning against the wall, her breathing fast. Oh god. This was serious. I ran up to her, reaching out and resting a hand on her shoulder. "Bristol?" She had to answer. She couldn't leave me.

"Sutton?" I heard footsteps behind me and Michael's voice. His hand rested on my shoulder. "What's going on?"

Bristol shook her head, glancing from me to Michael and back again. "I don't know," I said, hearing the words like they were coming from someone else. "But I have to get Bristol out of here. I have to take her to the hospital."

Michael looked from me back to Bristol, then just nodded. He dug his car keys out of his pocket and passed them to me. "Take my car. I'll tell your parents and come join you, okay?"

I didn't even know how to say thank you to him. I just squeezed his hands, taking the car keys. "Okay."

"Can you walk?" I asked, turning towards Bristol.

She took another breath, her whole body trembling. "It's just – it's a panic attack."

This didn't look like a panic attack to me. She couldn't breathe. I couldn't leave my sister like this. "Let's go. I'm taking you to the hospital."

She nodded. That was all that I needed. Michael looked over at the two of us, then looped his arm around Bristol. "Do you need any help walking?"

And with the two of us, we wrapped our arms around Bristol and walked with her out to Michael's car. I unlocked the door and slid Bristol into the passenger seat. "Thank you," I said, my words coming out in a whisper.

He shook his head. "If Bristol needs the doctor, you take her, okay? Don't worry about anything." He squeezed my hands before I shut the door and started the car.

I drove out of the parking lot as fast as I could. I hit Mia's number in my phone, turning the phone on speaker as we drove towards the local hospital.

"Sutton? Is everything okay?" Mia's voice asked.

I could have sworn that Bristol's breathing even seemed to slow down at the sound of Mia's voice. "I don't think so." No, that wasn't true. "No, it's not."

"Okay, tell me what's going on." Mia's voice was fast and low.

"We were at this thing with my parents, and they asked Bristol to speak, and she just – she's trembling and breathing really fast and I don't know what to do. We're going to the hospital," I said. I almost missed a turn and slammed on the brakes, whipping the car to the left.

"Okay." Mia took a deep breath on the other end. "She's having a panic attack."

I didn't think a panic attack looked like this. This

was too serious for this. "She's breathing so fast, Mia. She's not even talking to me."

"I know." Mia's voice was still steady. "This used to happen a lot at school. She doesn't need a doctor, but she needs us to help her. Can you start counting to five for her?"

"What?" No way was that enough. Mia wasn't here, and I wasn't risking losing my sister. We were going to the ER.

"Put me on speaker." Mia waited for a second, then I heard her voice. "Brizzy. It's me. Breathe with me, okay?"

I tuned out Mia as much as I could, trying to drive. "One, two, three, four, five," I heard Mia count on the other end. "Breathe with me."

We pulled up to the hospital, and I came to a screeching halt in front of the building. "Mia, I'm going to the hospital with her," I said into the phone.

"Okay, let me keep talking to her, though," Mia said, and I passed Bristol the phone. "Bristol, you're holding a phone right now. It's kind of heavy and kind of warm," Mia continued, her voice smooth.

I grabbed Bristol's hand and helped her out of the car, towards the hospital. We limped through the front doors, and I looked up at the front desk. "My sister is – is this a panic attack?"

"Tell them that Bristol needs a wet washcloth.

It helps her with the sensory stuff," Mia said over the phone. Her voice was drowned out by the doors behind us, and I took my own deep breath. They had to help Bristol. I couldn't do this all by myself.

The nurse at the front desk took one look at us and nodded. "Okay. We've got this."

She led us into a small room off the side, and Bristol said down in one of the chairs. "We're going to get you a washcloth, okay? Just keep taking deep breaths."

My own breathing started to slow down. We were at the hospital. Someone was going to take care of us, someone who knew enough about medicine and health and could help Bristol out of this. I didn't know what else to do.

We sat there for just long enough that I could hear Bristol's breathing start to slow down. She closed her eyes for a second, looking over towards me. "I'm – "

I stared at her for a second. "You scared me so much."

She swallowed, closing her eyes again for a second. "This is what happens when you have a panic attack. It feels like you're having a heart attack."

I swallowed. "I overreacted, didn't I?"

She looked at me for a second. "I mean, yeah, but I'm glad you did."

"Sutton!" Natalie stormed through the door, Nora and Stacey right behind her. "Bristol! Are you all okay?"

"What?" I stared up at them. How had they known? "What are you doing here?"

"Michael called us," Stacey said, edging through the door. "And hi, Bristol."

I looked over at Michael, who followed them into the room, his hands stuck into his pockets. He was still in his button down from the event, looking too handsome for the hospital. "Sorry," he said, looking around the room. He took a step towards me, resting his hand on my shoulder. "I told everyone, and they had to come."

"And we obviously weren't going to not come once we heard that you and Bristol were at the hospital!" Natalie said, shaking her head. It seemed like she'd been in the middle of braiding her hair when she'd gotten the call, one braid swinging.

"And somebody had to drive Michael, because he was really worried and didn't have a car," Stacey added.

Bristol closed her eyes for a second. "Well, hi, everyone."

"Are we being embarrassing?" Nora asked, looking around. "Sorry, Bristol."

Bristol snorted. "I should have known this would happen. At least you're not my old coach."

"That was terrible of them to do," Michael said, his voice tense. I turned towards him.

"You mean to tell me that I was supposed to speak at that thing?" Bristol swallowed. "Michael. I really respected your dad. He was one of the people who got that it was supposed to be about having fun at sports."

Michael swallowed. "He would have lost it to see what happened tonight. He always told me that it was the most important thing to love the things and people in your life. That if you didn't love a sport any more, it was time to leave it. He would never have wanted you to be the best if it meant that you felt this way."

Bristol stared at Michael for a second. "Coach Shipman was a good person."

Michael nodded, his eyes starting to get slightly wet. He closed them for a second, looking away from us. "He used to tell me that love was enough when you were in the right thing. And if love wasn't enough, it meant that the sport or the person wasn't right for you. If you're done with lacrosse, it just means that there's room for something else in your heart."

And just then, there was another rustle at the door. "Bristol!"

It was my parents, standing there, their mouths open. "Is everything okay?"

I looked down at Bristol, my hand wrapping around hers. "Maybe not yet," I said, "but it's going to be."

"I can't believe that they're actually closing for the winter this year," Natalie said, taking a giant lick of her ice cream.

"I can't believe that you're making me eat this," Nora said, looking down at her lobster bisque ice cream. It might have been the same one that I'd had at the beginning of the summer, because it turned out that lobster bisque was not a popular ice cream flavor.

"Eat up," Natalie said, sticking her tongue out.

"I'm so glad that I got out of doing the bucket list with you this summer," Stacey said, taking a bite of her own, relatively normal rocky road ice cream.

We were all sitting at Brittany's on the last day of the summer, looking out over the water. In the rush of the summer, we'd forgotten to complete every flavor, and today was the official end of the bucket list.

Somehow, I'd managed to cross off every item, even the ones that had seemed impossible at the beginning of the summer. And beyond that, I'd even added my own. *Fall in love*, and *find my best friends*.

"Are you going to come out with us to see Marcus's concert?" Natalie asked, turning towards me. Somehow, Marcus seemed to be one of the longer lived of Natalie's relationships, and she had turned into an unofficial groupie and band manager for Marcus's garage band.

"I can't. I told Bristol that I would help her move." I took another bite of my ice cream. Mint chocolate chip, which Nora had told me to keep far away from her.

"Oh, right," Stacey said, looking over at me. "That'll be a fun trip."

I nodded. After a lot of discussion and plenty of sessions with Bristol's college therapist, my parents had agreed that Bristol should stop playing lacrosse. She was moving in with Mia at an off-campus apartment, but taking classes at the local community college and spending a lot of time in therapy. It was technically a year off from college, but it was the best that I'd ever seen Bristol.

My parents had finally broken down and

admitted that Bristol needed more than being at home. She'd found a new therapist who was licensed both here and at school and finally started the medication her college therapist had given her. She wasn't magically better, but she seemed to be getting better and better every day.

It had taken my parents getting a call from the hospital to let them know that Bristol was there that had done it. They'd realized that we were going to lose Bristol from our family if we didn't know how to support her, and after a lot of crying and discussions, we were finally on the right track.

We weren't there yet. There were still going to be tough parts, but that was okay. For the first time, I could look around and know that even if I didn' know who I wanted to be, I was going to get there. And most importantly, I had the people I wanted to do it with.

Even if that meant that sometimes, we'd eat the worst ice cream in the world on the way.

ABOUT THE AUTHOR

Caroline Hopkins has been writing books since high school, when she discovered that writing stories was much more fun than taking notes. When she's not reading or writing, she's either spending time in the mountains, going for a slow run, or catering to the whims of one very spoiled cat.

ALSO BY CAROLINE HOPKINS

Summer Off Script

www.ingramcontent.com/pod-product-compliance
Lightning Source LLC
Chambersburg PA
CBHW030123010826
48973CB00002B/402